Hunting Moon

A Decorah Security Novel

Decorah Security Series, Book #11
A Paranormal Romantic Suspense Novel

By Rebecca York

Ruth Glick writing as Rebecca York

Published by Light Street Press
Copyright © 2016 by Ruth Glick
Cover design by Earthly Charms

ISBN: 978-1-943191-00-0.

CHAPTER ONE

The last thing Tory Robinson expected to hear was the sound of gunshots.

She'd been sitting on the comfortable couch in Johnny Denato's luxury Central Park South condo. When he'd excused himself to take a business call, she'd walked to the outsized living room windows to enjoy the ten million dollar view of the park.

Behind her, a door opened, and she heard Denato's voice change abruptly. Someone must have come in, and he was demanding to know what they wanted. As the voices grew louder, she whirled around in time to hear a series of popping noises and catch a quick view of men with guns running past the living room door.

Fear threatened to turn her body to stone. But she knew that if she stayed where she was, she was a dead woman. Dropping to the floor behind the sofa, she crawled toward the heavy drapes that pooled at either side of the window and worked her way behind the nearest panel. Praying that the gunmen were still in the back of the apartment, she eased to a standing position and pressed against the wall, the cold plaster raising goose bumps on her arms.

Her mind's eye flashed to the coffee table in front of the sofa where she and Denato had been sitting. He had left a glass of bourbon on the glass top, but she'd told him she

1

didn't want a drink. So an extra glass wouldn't give her away. And thank God she'd taken her purse with her. The men wouldn't see that two people had been in the room—unless they noticed two depressions in the back sofa cushions.

Voices conferred in low tones, the words like the roaring of surf in her ears. When heavy footsteps approached the window, the blood froze in her veins, and she braced to feel rough hands shove the drapes aside and yank her out like a rabbit plucked from its burrow.

An eternity ticked by before she heard a sarcastic voice say, "High class view."

"It won't do him no good now," another man answered.

"We better get the hell out of here, in case somebody heard the action."

"Right."

As footsteps receded from the window, Tory closed her eyes and leaned her head against the wall, taking deep breaths as she ordered herself not to faint. For long seconds after the front door closed, she stayed where she was, imagining that the gunmen could be waiting to see if someone crept out of hiding.

But finally she knew she couldn't stay where she was.

Cautiously, she eased one edge of the drapes aside and looked out. The apartment was just as she remembered it—until she saw a pair of black-trouser-clad legs lying on the marble floor of the foyer.

She recognized Johnny's dress pants—and his Italian designer shoes.

"Johnny?" she whispered, hurrying toward him, stopping short when she saw the red circle in the middle of his forehead and the pool of blood that had spread around his head like an evil halo against the pale floor. There was nothing she could do for him now.

The seafood dinner she'd eaten threatened to come up as she hurried around him and toward the door of the apartment. She stopped short as she reached the exit.

"Think," she whispered to herself.

She'd been raised to be an upstanding citizen, which meant that she should call the police. But she was sure that this murder wouldn't go unreported for long. Better to clear out before the cops came and started asking her questions— and she ended up on the front page of the *New York Times*, with the murderers wondering what she'd seen. Which was nothing, except Johnny's body. The drapes that had hidden her had completely blocked her view of the assassins.

She always carried a scarf in her purse. Taking it out, she put it on her head and tied it under her chin, then pulled it forward to hide her blond hair and her forehead.

She'd come in through the lobby, but the man at the front desk hadn't paid her any attention. And Johnny Denato probably brought in leggy blonds all the time.

He'd seemed like a ladies' man, although his behavior with her had certainly been odd since she'd first spotted him watching her performance at the Midnight Club. When he'd asked her to his table after the show, she'd assumed he wanted sex. But he'd told her he'd admired her dancing and would like to spend a little time with her. He'd been charming and smart, and her boss had told her to be nice to him.

Still, because she knew he had an underworld reputation, she'd only reluctantly let him take her to dinner after the last performance. Although they'd been out a few times since that first evening, she'd never agreed to go to his apartment before. Tonight he'd said he needed to pick up a fax from a business associate. Now she knew she should have said good night and taken a cab home from the restaurant.

Or to be honest, she should have gone back to Pittsburgh where she belonged—before getting involved with a guy like Denato. Unfortunately, after scoring a featured spot in the Midnight Club review, she'd tried to convince herself that she could deal with big-city life and a boss who was constantly demanding more.

But there was no use beating herself up for previous decisions. She had to deal with *now*.

Should she take the stairs to a back exit? That might keep her out of the lobby, but there were sure to be cameras in the stairwells.

After weighing the pros and cons, she walked across the hallway to the elevator, keeping her head down to hide her face from the camera in the ceiling as she took the car to the first floor.

Her heart clanged inside her chest all the way down. Just before the door opened, an idea struck. Taking out her cell phone, she pretended to be deep into texting someone as she walked smartly past the desk at the side of the room and out the front entrance, avoiding the doorman's eye.

She half expected someone to call her back or, worse yet, clamp a hand on her shoulder. But no one interfered as she hurried down the block toward the hotel on the corner.

Before she reached it, she saw a cab slowing to let off a passenger. The man who'd occupied the backseat brushed past her, as she climbed in.

"Where to?"

She gave her address in Brooklyn, then leaned back and closed her eyes, her heart rate slowing a little. She'd made a lucky escape, at least for now. But she wasn't going to feel safe until she was on her way out of the city.

Brand Marshall stood in the wooded area near his home in upper Montgomery County, Maryland, taking in the scents and rustles of the forest. At the moment his appreciation of the natural setting was dulled by his humanity. Soon it would be different.

As he unbuttoned his shirt and laid it on top of his shoes and socks, he stared into the darkness, anticipation of his night's adventure coursing through him. When he had shed the trappings of civilization, he closed his dark eyes, the better to focus on ancient ritual and ancient deities as he gathered his inner strength, steeling himself for the feeling of disorientation, even as he said the words that would change him from man to wolf.

"*Taranis, Epona, Cerridwen,*" he said in a low voice, then repeated the same phrase and went on to another that had been a part of his consciousness for almost fifteen years.

"Ga. Feart. Cleas. Duais. Aithriocht. Go gcumhdai is dtreorai na deithe thu."

With the words came a blinding pain that had killed one of his older brothers. Brand had been luckier. On that night of first transformation, he had become more than a man. Or less, if you agreed with the monster hunters of ages past.

He'd been giddy with relief that he'd survived the change from teen to wolf. It took a few years for him to understand that he'd given up as much as he'd gained.

The words of the ancient chant had helped him through the agony of first transformation, opened his mind, and freed him from the bonds of the human shape. Since then, he had tried more than once to watch it happen in a mirror, but his vision had blurred as if his soul must reject that which was beyond a mortal's comprehension.

Still, he could picture it in his mind. Even as the human part of his being screamed in protest, he felt his jaw elongate, his teeth sharpen, his body contort as muscles and limbs transformed themselves into a different shape.

The first few times he'd done it had been a nightmare of torture and terror. Once he'd understood what to expect, he'd learned to ride above the physical sensations of bones crunching, muscles jerking, his very cells changing from one shape to another.

Thick gray hair formed along his flanks, covering his body in a silver-tipped pelt. The color—the very structure—of his eyes changed as he dropped to all fours. No longer a man but an animal far more suited to the forest around him.

A wolf.

As he drank in the rich scents of the night, a surge of freedom rippled through him. His wolf's lips drew back in a smile as he pawed the ground with the joy of a creature totally at one with nature. Raising his head, he looked around with keener vision, pricked his ears for sounds his human senses had been unable to detect.

His body quivered. The blood sang hotly in his veins. He fought the impulse to throw back his head and howl into the night for the sheer joy of it. But he stayed the urge, because the mind inside his skull still held his human intelligence. And the man understood that the cry of a wolf in the night would be out of place in the Maryland suburbs. Hunting here could be only a temporary respite.

He was restless. He needed more. He knew he had to get away—to a place where his wolf's body was free to break the rules mankind had imposed on it.

CHAPTER TWO

When the cab pulled up in front of Tory's apartment building, she took a moment to look around at the darkened street, probing the shadows, wishing she had the night vision of a nocturnal animal. She saw nothing, but would she see anything before it was too late?

Skewered by that comforting thought, she paid the driver and gave him a generous tip before exiting the cab and walking rapidly to her front door. Unlike Johnny Denato's building, there was no doorman and no staff in the front lobby. Only a row of mailboxes attached to the walls in the grimy, narrow hallway.

Out of habit, she checked her mail, thinking she wasn't going to leave a forwarding address.

Like a drowning victim she felt her life flash before her eyes as she climbed the stairs to her apartment.

She'd grown up in the Pittsburgh suburbs, with a stay-at-home mom and a dad who worked for the state government. They'd encouraged her to take whatever classes she wanted when she was a grade-schooler and teenager. Dancing, especially modern dance, had been her passion, and she'd determined to give that career a shot. She'd been elated to get a place in the Midnight Club's chorus line, knowing it had as much to do with her looks as her dancing ability. But the job hadn't satisfied her as much as she'd thought it would, and she'd been about to accept her friend Penny Wayne's offer to come back home and teach at her dance studio.

At her door, she opened three locks, another thing she hated about the city.

As soon as she'd stepped inside, she realized she was making a mistake. She couldn't just run away and let someone else worry about Johnny Denato's murder—much as she longed to simply disappear. That was morally wrong. Plus she and Johnny had been seen together tonight at the club between shows. And later at dinner at the Four Seasons. The cops would be tracking his movements, and people would remember him with a tall, blue-eyed blond.

She was just reaching for the phone to call the police and tell them she'd panicked and left Denato's apartment, when she heard someone clomping up the stairs. Either one of the neighbors was coming home late—or it was an unwanted visitor.

The breath froze in her lungs as she waited to find out which.

Then a knock at the door made her feel like someone had pushed her off the edge of a steep cliff into a whirlwind.

"Police, open up."

Yeah, right, she thought as she struggled to recover from free fall. Like the cops would know to come look for her less than half an hour after Denato had been shot. People might remember her face, but they wouldn't know her name.

She tiptoed toward the door and tried to look through the peephole, but someone had pressed a finger over it. A good clue that it wasn't the authorities in the hall.

There was another loud knock. "Police, open up."

"Just a minute. I'm not dressed." She dashed into the bedroom, pulling her phone from her purse and dialing 911. Nobody would get here in time to rescue her, but at least they'd know she was in trouble.

When she heard a woman answer, she started to shout for help. Then she heard, "All our lines are busy. Please hold."

8

With a grimace, she clicked off and slung the purse strap across her chest before whirling toward the window and pushing up the sash. The building next to hers was a story lower, and she'd always hated the view of the gravel roof. Now she thanked God for the escape route as she threw a leg over the window ledge, then climbed out and turned around, stretching out her arms so that she could lower herself to the rough surface. Her dancer's muscles were strong, and she eased herself down. Still, her grip faltered when she heard a loud crash behind her that must be someone caving in her front door. As she landed on her knees on the sharp stones, she clenched her teeth to keep from crying out.

Desperately, she righted herself, then lit out toward the little structure that housed the stairwell of the building, praying that the door was unlocked.

It was, and she pelted down the stairs, then to the alley entrance, where she emerged onto a parking pad in back. Once at ground level, she slowed her pace, creeping along the side of a car until she could look out into the alley.

It was clear, and she ran toward the street, not even breathing hard as she rounded the corner. A muscular man wearing a knit shirt and jeans was coming toward her, the look in his eyes telling her that he wasn't a friend.

Abruptly reversing course, she started back the other way, only to find another guy who could have been his twin blocking her retreat. The only way to go was down a side passage, but a car door opened, and a third man leaped out, all of them making a circle around her.

Her gaze darted from one to the other as she tensed, ready to deliver a blow to any of them that who got close.

But one circled around and grabbed her from behind. When she kicked back at his ankle, he made a grunting sound. As she tried to twist out of his grip, he slapped a wet cloth over her face, and that was the last thing she knew as blackness closed in.

CHAPTER THREE

"Come in," Frank Decorah called from behind his wide desk.

Brand stepped into the small but well-appointed office, once again struck by how youthful his boss looked. He was in his sixties, with salt and pepper hair, but a limber body and features remarkable for a man of his age.

The former SEAL had lost part of a leg in Vietnam and come home to the Naval Medical Center for rehab. After that, he'd gone into PI work, first for a local agency before branching out on his own. He was one of the best in the business, with sometimes astonishing perceptions.

"Have a seat," Frank said, laying down the gold eagle coin that he'd been turning in his hand.

Brand pulled out one of the guest chairs and sat.

"So what's this about? Is guard duty at our new bio facility too tame for you?" Frank asked, referring to the lab where Dr. Lily Bradley was caring for comatose patients with special needs.

Brand blinked. "I haven't been performing satisfactorily?"

Frank leaned back comfortably in his chair. "Your work has been fine. You were outstanding at the Hamilton Lab's takedown. I'm just responding to the vibes you've been giving off lately. You want some time off?"

Brand wasn't surprised that his boss had picked up on his restlessness. "Uh-huh."

"How much do you need?"

Brand lifted one shoulder. "I'm not sure. "He didn't say his present mood might also have something to do with reaching the age of werewolf bonding.

"And hopefully you'll come back ready for duty."

Brand nodded.

"When do you want to leave?"

"Now. If that's okay."

Frank didn't miss a beat. "Yes, fine. I can shuffle some assignments around. Where are you going? Off to the Caribbean like Rafe?" he asked, referring to another one of the Decorah agents who had departed for an island vacation and ended up in the middle of a terrorist attack—where he had rescued the woman who became his lifemate.

Brand was hoping for a much more peaceful hiatus. "I like the north woods."

"How far north?"

"Upstate New York."

"Sounds reasonable. Stay out of trouble."

Brand tipped his head to the side, studying Frank Decorah, considering the way he'd delivered that last line.

"You think I'm going to step into something unexpected?"

"Yeah."

"Why?"

"Just a feeling I have."

Brand nodded. Frank was like that. He hired agents who had special powers, but he seemed to have them as well, although Brand had never figured out exactly what psychic talents his boss possessed. He didn't seem like the shape-shifter type. Did he dream about the future like Wyatt Granger, one of the other Decorah Agents? Know when a client was going to need their special services? Frank had a way of anticipating someone's next move, and he was rarely wrong. Like at the Hamilton Labs, where he'd had the team

11

stick around instead of leaving when it looked like the emergency was over.

"Call if you need us," Frank said.

"I will," Brand answered, wondering what, exactly, he was going to need.

CHAPTER FOUR

Tory's eyes blinked open. Her head felt like little men were inside her skull, pounding on it from the inside with tiny hammers. For a moment she couldn't figure out where the headache had come from—or where she was, for that matter.

She lay very still, trying to get her bearings. She seemed to be in some kind of moving vehicle. A car?

When she tried to rise up and look around, the effort sent a wave of sickness crashing through her, and she fell back against a lumpy surface. Closing her eyes helped. Still she knew she was hanging on to consciousness—or maybe it was sanity—by her fingernails.

Something bad had happened. But what? The gap in her memory made her heart pound and cold sweat break out on her body. She gasped in air, then struggled for calm.

Think, she ordered herself. You can't panic. Think.

When she did capture a memory, it was like grabbing onto a live electric wire. An image sizzled behind her closed eyes— a man lying on the floor, blood spreading around his head. His name followed the awful picture. Johnny Denato. She'd been in his condo when men had come in and shot him.

The next part was just as bad. She'd run, bent on getting out of the city before anyone figured out that she'd been there. But it was already too late.

A goon squad had come after her. And now?

She choked back the scream welling up in her throat. Maybe if they didn't realize she was awake, she could get away. And then what? She didn't even know where she was. But she had to try to escape, because she understood in the part of her brain still capable of rational thinking that the unknown was better than the here and now.

She took several calming breaths as she assessed her physical situation. Nothing hurt besides her head and the palms of her hands where the roof gravel had dug into them. Or to put it more directly, the men who had captured her hadn't done anything to harm her after they'd drugged her. At least that was encouraging. On the other hand, her wrists were secured in front of her. Slitting her eyes, she studied the bonds and saw one of those plastic handcuff things.

When she heard a door open, then footsteps approaching, she tried to relax, willing herself not to tense up as she imagined one of the hard-faced men standing over her.

"She still out cold?" a voice inquired.

"Far as I can tell."

She forced herself not to react when a large hand grasped her shoulder and shook her.

She heard his breathing, but he said nothing more as he remained where he was for several heartbeats, then turned around and withdrew.

Her mind circled back to the problem of where she was— exactly. In a van? She could feel the vehicle moving, more up and down than from side to side. The movement didn't seem like a car.

She focused on the odd motion, then choked back a gasp when she realized where she must be. In a plane. Oh Lord— they were flying her somewhere. North? South?

All she knew was that they were in a hurry to get her away from the city.

She struggled to hold back the sob trying to claw its way up her throat. As she clenched her fists, she tried to plan her escape. Cracking her eyelids, she looked around in the dim light. She was in a low, narrow compartment, hardly high enough to stand up. A small plane. There were no windows in the immediate area, and only a dim overhead light made it possible to see anything. It looked like she was in a cargo hold, only it couldn't be like the hold where they put the luggage on a big aircraft, because then she'd be freezing cold, wouldn't she? No, this was simply the back of a small plane, where someone had thrown a thin mattress for her to lie on.

Cautiously, she sat up, then began looking for some way to free her hands. The bulkheads were unadorned metal. Working by touch, she found a sharp place where two seams joined. After a quick glance at the forward door, she raised her hands and began sawing the thick plastic band back and forth over the protruding metal, praying that the guy who had come to check on her wasn't going to come back and see what she was doing. Progress seemed to take forever, but she figured out that if she angled her hands, she could make a notch in one side, then a larger cut.

When she felt a shift in the way the aircraft was flying, she knew they must be getting ready for a landing. The band wasn't quite cut through yet, but maybe that was good. It was almost done, and if she turned the cut side inward, she should be able to hide her progress.

As the plane kept descending, she laid down again, drawing her knees up and her head down, pretending she was out of it but preparing herself to escape when she got the chance.

They touched down none too smoothly and bounced along a runway before braking to a stop. Then she heard the door at the front open again, and a man come through. Probably the same guy who had checked on her before.

"Come on," he said. "Time to get up."

She made a moaning sound.

"You awake?"

When she didn't answer, he shook her. "Awake?"

"Sort of," she mumbled.

He opened a hatch in the bulkhead, and she saw dim light outside. It looked like early morning. Did that mean they'd been flying for the rest of the night—or had they not taken off right away?

"Give me a hand," he called out.

Another man—probably the pilot—came from the front, and together they muscled her down a short flight of steps that had swung out when the hatch opened. They set her on her feet, and she wavered as they held her up, pretending she was weaker than she really was as she looked around.

She saw a stretch of tarmac, a couple of buildings to her right, and beyond that, trees.

A small rural airport? Did the people running the place know there was a kidnap victim arriving, or didn't they give a damn?

"Looks like our ride is here." The man who had first come to check on her pointed to a long black car parked at the side of the runway. A Lincoln Town Car or something similar. "Let me make sure it's him."

The man who had spoken left her with the pilot, and she watched him stride across the blacktop. The other guy held her only loosely, and she tried not to telegraph her intentions as she waited for her chance.

Suddenly she rammed her elbow into his side. As he grunted in pain, she wrenched away and lit out in the opposite direction from the car.

She might have been unconscious a little while ago, but she had an athlete's stamina and legs.

Ignoring the shout behind her, she yanked at the plastic strip holding her wrists, pulling through the last of the bond as she headed for a low clapboard-sided structure, making decisions as she sprinted. The logical thing would be to go inside and ask for help, but in this case she was sure that was the wrong tactic. Her captors had deliberately chosen an isolated location. If she ran into the building, she could be trapping herself, or whoever was in there could grab her.

16

Veering to the right, she ducked around the building, making for the woods. She was stopped by a high chain-link fence, topped with razor wire.

Tory didn't waste any energy on a cry of frustration. She simply changed directions, running along the barrier, praying she'd come to an open gate. Behind her she could hear the men from the plane and maybe another one. The driver of the luxury car or someone from the building.

She kept going, the air wheezing in and out of her lungs. Ahead of her she saw an entrance to the airport—and an open gate. If she could only make it through, she could disappear into the woods.

But she never reached that haven. One of the men behind her must have realized that he was in serious danger of losing her and put on a desperate burst of speed. Grabbing her by the shoulder, he threw her to the ground.

When she tried to roll away, he smacked her hard across the face, stunning her.

"Bitch."

He had pulled back his hand to sock her in the mouth when the other guy caught up with them and grabbed the assailant's hand.

"Don't damage her."

"She ..."

"Leave her be."

The one who had spoken knelt beside her, then swore when he saw that she'd freed her hands.

"Tricky," he muttered as he pulled another set of plastic handcuffs from his back pocket and secured her wrists again.

"Please, let me go."

"Can't do that. Come on."

He hauled her to her feet and led her back the way they'd come.

She wanted to scream or sob, but she wasn't going to give these guys the satisfaction. One on either side, they gripped her arms as they marched her back toward the long black car.

A back door opened, and a man she hadn't seen before got out. Slender except for signs of pudginess around his middle, he was wearing a dark suit with a white shirt and a subdued red tie. His dark hair was neatly combed, and his face was pale, as though he didn't go out much. He looked like he was in his mid-forties, and he could have been dressed for an evening at the Midnight Club—or the symphony.

"I'm Dr. Raymond," he said.

"Who?"

"Dr. Raymond. I'll be working with you."

"Why? I don't need you to work with me. I'm fine."

"Not if you're so paranoid that you needed to try and escape."

He looked around at the open-air setting. "This isn't a good place to talk. We can have a nice chat when we get to the Refuge."

"Paranoid? Your guys just drugged me and flew me away from New York City to God knows where."

"For your own good. You'll have to trust me on that."

"Oh, right."

As his men held her in place, he took a quick step forward. When he lifted his arm, she saw a hypodermic in his hand, then felt the prick of the needle. Lord, not again.

Only seconds later, she felt her vision and her mind begin to blur, and she would have fallen over if the men hadn't been holding her up.

"Let's get her into the car," Raymond said.

At first, she didn't actually lose consciousness, but all her senses and her mind felt like they had been coated with a layer of thick, sticky foam.

One of the men got into the front of the car behind the wheel. The doctor got in back with her, speaking in a soothing voice, telling her that she was safe now, that she'd been too upset to know what she was doing, that she should trust him to take care of her.

Trust him?

A laugh bubbled in her throat.

She fought against the hypnotic sound of his voice, but the drug he'd given her was leaching away the ability to think clearly.

"You're feeling disoriented?" he asked in a soothing voice that made her want to scream.

"Yes," she managed to say.

"Just relax. Let yourself go. We'll get you to the Refuge, and you'll be safe. You'll get the care you need there."

She didn't need any care, and somewhere in her confused mind, she was cursing herself for not going straight to the police as soon she'd found Denato's body.

CHAPTER FIVE

As Brand drove north, he felt a strange excitement building inside his chest. It made him think of the first giddy moments when he'd well and truly changed from man to wolf. He had survived the fierce, paralyzing headache and come through the test—alive.

And when he'd glanced at his father, he saw the tremendous relief on his face. That look almost paralyzed Brand again because it suddenly jolted him to the realization that Dad had come here prepared to bring home another dead son. But this time the ancient gods had granted mercy to the Marshall family.

To celebrate, Dad took Brand on a hunting trip to the Finger Lakes National Forest. It was one of the best memories of his life—alone with the old man, learning the skills he'd need to live as a werewolf.

Of course, there were plenty of learning opportunities when he was growing up. His family lived in an ideal location for a werewolf pack—a farm in western Howard County, Maryland, where they could have the privacy they needed to hunt—and no noisy neighbors to ask why two of their teenage boys, seemingly the picture of health, had died suddenly.

The Marshalls raised sheep, which helped fulfil their need for meat. Dad also brought in money running a rural machinery repair shop where local farmers brought equipment that had broken down.

But the most memorable week of Brand's teen years was that trip north, just the two of them.

Today he was going there again, as an adult.

His memories of that first trip were vivid. The two of them hiking to a secluded area. Dad showing him how to dig a trench around their tent so it wouldn't flood in a rainstorm. Dad pointing out which plants a human could eat and showing him how to rappel down one of the many cliffs in the area. And the two of them working together to herd a deer into a blind canyon.

Now he'd supplemented those memories with research about the natural area and found it lay on a ridge—called the Hector Backbone—between Seneca and Cayuga Lakes. New York State's only national forest, it was patterned after similar parks out west, with great sweeps of open land as well as thick forest stands.

He was going there for a wolf's hunt, but he saw the wisdom of establishing a human campsite, the way his father had done.

After setting out before dawn, he'd made the trip north in five hours and was caught by a sense of homecoming as he found a secluded parking area where he could leave his vehicle. Intent on getting as far away from civilization as possible, he shouldered his pack and set off into the wilderness. A man might have worried about finding his way back to where he'd left his vehicle. A werewolf had no such problem.

He followed a trail through thick forest, then crossed a meadow and plunged into forest again, this time without a path to follow, which was what he'd been looking for.

Two hours later, he figured he was far enough from the world of men. Picking a clearing at the edge of a hard wood grove, he set up his tent near a stream where he could get fresh water. Once he had secured the camp site, he grew restless, ready to change to wolf form and prowl.

He'd told himself he was coming to this secluded location to get away from his normal routine. Now he was wondering why he was really here.

He should relax and wait for dark before he changed, but he couldn't make himself hold back. He stomped off into a blackberry thicket and started taking off his clothes, too impatient to fold anything neatly before he rushed into the chant that would change him from man to wolf.

The transformation grabbed him in a way he hadn't expected. It was like a new burst of freedom.

Still, he was cautious as he made his way through the woods, wary of running into a hunter who would love the chance to bring home a wolf-pelt trophy. If someone shot and killed him in wolf form, would he stay that way? It was a question that had run through his mind on some of his Decorah assignments.

Then he'd often been on a dangerous assignment. Was he operating as a wolf now because he wanted to take a risk?

He slipped through the forest, listening to the sounds of the wildlife around him, passing a small herd of deer, breathing in their fear as they became aware of him. But he would only hunt after dark.

Instead he headed north, sensing that something was drawing him. He had the impulse to fight it. But he shook it off because his destiny was here in these woods.

It was fanciful notion that reminded him of a book he'd read a long time ago—*Appointment in Samarra*—about a man who tries to outrun death but finds it waiting for him anyway.

Was death stalking Brand? He had the feeling it was something else entirely. More like life.

Or the life he was meant to lead. Did that mean he wasn't coming back to Decorah Security?

He hoped that wasn't the case.

CHAPTER SIX

"How are you feeling this evening?"

Tory opened her eyes and tried to focus on ... Dr. Raymond, the man who had brought her to this place a little while ago.

What had he called it? A name, "The Refuge," bobbed to the surface of her mind like a fishing cork in murky lake water.

Tory was sitting in a comfortable chair, her head lolling to the side. Gripping the padded arms of the chair, she pushed herself up straighter, blinking as she took in the doctor and then the room.

Raymond was relaxing in a similar chair, separated from her by a small oval table. There was a large rosewood desk across from them, a tasteful Oriental rug on the floor, and light wood paneling on the walls. The room was about twelve by thirteen feet, she judged, and the window behind the desk had bars. The only other furnishing was a sideboard, like the kind that held lateral file drawers. There were no ornaments in sight, probably so that she couldn't pick up an ashtray and bash the doctor's head in. And escape? She didn't even know what was behind the closed door.

Last time she'd seen this man was in the car where the nicely dressed goons had taken her. Then the doctor had been wearing a business suit. Now he had on a more casual outfit, dark slacks and a light blue golf shirt.

"How are you feeling?" he repeated, closing the notebook he must have been writing in. She'd like to see those notes.

"I don't know," she answered uncertainly.

"You have these spells," the doctor said.

She tried to work her way through the statement—and the implications. "Spells?" she repeated cautiously, fighting the icy fear that was collecting in the pit of her stomach like slush on the side of a highway in winter.

"Yes. Sometimes you're perfectly lucid and other times you seem to go off into never-never land.

Again, Tory tried to make sense of his words. "What do you mean, sometimes?" she asked in a barely audible voice when she wanted to scream.

"Last week we thought you were making good progress, but you seem to have slid back downhill."

"Last week? I just got here," she shot back.

The doctor's expression turned sympathetic as he shook his head. "You didn't just arrive. You've been at the Refuge for three weeks."

"No! Men brought me up here in a plane..." She fought against rising panic as she turned her head toward the window and saw that it was dark outside. "I guess it had to be yesterday. I tried to get away, but they caught me and brought me to you in the car."

Raymond shook his head sadly. "You keep coming back to that incident in our sessions, but it wasn't yesterday. It was three weeks ago."

Denial was her only defense. "No! I don't believe you. That's a mistake—or a trick."

She pushed herself up and stood on shaky legs, then looked down at her clothing. She had come here wearing the dressy black sweater and skirt she'd changed into after work. Now she was wearing dark sweatpants and a yellow sweatshirt. The thought that someone had undressed her and dressed her again sent a shiver over her skin. She wanted to check to see if she had on the bra and panties that she'd been wearing, but she wasn't going to do that in front of this guy, not even if he really was a doctor.

"I know it's tempting, but you can't hold on to that illusion," he said, using the same gentle voice he had when they'd been in the car... a few hours ago. She knew she'd only been here a few hours, didn't she?

"You fell asleep during our session," the doctor said. "You keep doing that. Either there's something seriously wrong with you physically, or you're using it as a way to avoid confronting your problems. We should do some blood work in the morning and see if your labs are normal."

She tried to keep her voice steady as she asked, "And what are my problems, exactly?"

"You feel guilty about your part in Mr. Denato's death, and that's destabilized your grip on reality."

The words hit her with the force of rocks hurled by desperate street fighters.

"My part in his death?" she gasped out. "I had no part in his death. I was in the other room when it happened."

"But you admit you were there?"

It was a question she didn't want to answer, but she settled for a small shrug.

"If you remember that, you must remember ... other things."

"Like what?" she murmured.

"I was hoping you could tell me. Tell me about your associates."

This man wanted something from her, and she was damned if she was going to give it to him. Or perhaps she was damned either way, she thought with a shudder, then fought against the dizzying sensation the movement produced.

"Perhaps if you were more specific," she answered, trying to get a handle on what this was all about.

"You don't have to lie about anything. Who did the actual shooting?"

She managed not to scream at him to leave her alone. Her mind was spinning. This man was sitting there calmly telling her she'd been here for three weeks, although she was sure it couldn't be true. Or was she the one making things up because she didn't want to believe him, and a false version of reality would soothe her?

"I won't press you now."

"Oh goody."

"I don't need any more sarcasm from you, young lady."

She kept her gaze steady, and he was the one who looked away first. "You can go join the other patients for dinner."

Dinner? She wasn't hungry, but maybe it was better to cooperate while she tried to figure out what was going on in this place.

As soon as Tory stepped out of the office, Alexander Raymond stood and locked the door behind her, muttering a curse under his breath.

"Stupid, stupid. You don't need to be in such a hurry. You have the luxury of doing this right. And you'd *better* do it right," he added.

But he couldn't shake the conviction that he had less time than he'd figured on.

He dismissed that notion with a savage chop of his hand, wishing he could have delivered a chop to the back of the woman's neck. She was putting up a fight, and he wasn't used to resistance—particularly from an airhead nightclub dancer.

Well, she'd find out tomorrow who was the boss here. Especially when she got some of the drugged food into her system.

* * *

Tory found herself stepping into a waiting room with comfortable couches and magazines on the table. She thought about looking at the dates for a clue to the real timeline here, but when had she ever found up-to-date reading material in a doctor's office?

A woman who looked to be in her mid to late forties was sitting on one of the couches reading a book. She put it down and turned toward the door that had opened. Her hair was a close cropped, faded brown. Her glasses were rimless, and she was wearing sweatpants like Tory's and a red sweatshirt.

"Hi," she said.

"Hi," Tory answered uncertainly.

"You asked me to wait for you."

"Did I?"

"Have you forgotten again?"

"I guess so."

"I'm June. We're friends."

She eyed the woman, sure that she had never seen her before, but she didn't challenge the claim that they knew and liked each other. "Okay."

June glanced toward the closed door. "I don't like the way he can be so rough on you—or maybe I meant me. But I guess it's part of the treatment."

Tory nodded. "Why are you here?"

"You mean at the Refuge?"

"Yes."

"We talked about that in therapy session."

"I don't remember."

"That's right. You keep forgetting stuff." The woman dragged in a breath and let it out. "I kind of went off the deep end after Earl and Tommy were killed. In a car crash," she added, with a gulp. "I was driving, and I was the only one who survived. We were coming back from an out-of-town trip. We should have stopped at a motel for the night, but I wanted to get back. It was late, and I think I fell asleep at the wheel."

"I'm sorry," Tory murmured. "Do you always talk about it compulsively?" she added, thinking that the explanation sounded like a well-rehearsed speech.

"You asked," the woman snapped, then seemed to remember who she was talking to. In a milder tone, she went on like she was repeating advice someone had given her—or repeating lines in a staged performance, "I have to learn to live with it—and go on with my life."

Tory could only give a little nod.

"The others are probably in the dining room," June said. "Let's go have something to eat."

"Okay," Tory answered, because it seemed safer to stick with this woman for the time being. She noted the route as they walked down a short hall, then turned to the right and entered a nicely decorated dining room with one large table like you might see in an upscale residence.

Two men were seated near the middle of the table. One looked like he was in his sixties, with gray hair fringing his bald head. The other was younger, maybe early fifties with small, suspicious eyes. Another woman, probably in her twenties, sat several places away from the men. Everyone at the table was wearing sweat clothes. And two more rough looking men dressed in golf shirts and jeans stood near the doors. They weren't the guys who had brought her here, but they were similar types. The people at the table looked up as Tory and June came in.

"Ted. Arthur. Robin," June said, pointing to each as she said their names.

They all nodded. Ted looked at her curiously. The others avoided eye contact. She wanted to ask what they were in here for, but she decided she'd wait until they volunteered something.

A waiter wearing a white shirt and dark slacks came in and began setting down plates. Ted got roast beef, a baked potato and green beans. Arthur got chicken with mashed potatoes and broccoli. Robin and June both had pasta with red sauce. A plate with the chicken entrée was set in front of Tory.

When she stared at it, the waiter said, "That's what you checked on your order sheet this morning. But we still have pasta with meat sauce, if you prefer."

"No. This is fine," she answered, determined not to rock the boat when none of this was making sense. She'd put in a dinner order this morning? And she'd been here for three weeks? She wanted to wrap her arms around her shoulders to ground herself, but she kept them at her sides. She wanted to ask one of the others how long she'd been at this place, but if they were in on the conspiracy, they'd give the same answer at Dr. Raymond.

Was it a conspiracy? For what purpose? To drive her crazy? Or to get information? If they thought she knew something she hadn't shared, they were in for a nasty surprise. Or perhaps *she* was. The thought sent another shiver over her skin.

The others ate in silence. Only June tried to engage Tory in conversation.

"Did they fix your hair dryer?" she asked.

"I don't know. Was it broken?"

"You said it was."

"Okay. I guess I'll find out if it was fixed."

"Are you coming to movie night?" June asked.

"What's playing?"

"You know. The Sound of Music."

"I think I'll pass. I'm kind of tired."

"I know the feeling," one of the men said, the one named Ted.

"How's your dinner?" she asked him.

He shrugged, and she went back to her meal.

The food was surprisingly good, not institutional at all, making Tory think that this was a pretty upscale insane asylum. Well, a private asylum, if that's what it really was.

Who was paying for it? She certainly didn't have the insurance for anything like this

She managed to eat about half her meal before the servers came back to take the plates away, then brought dessert.

The two men had ordered apple pie with vanilla ice cream. Tory and the other women were only having the ice cream. Strawberry for Tory and chocolate for June.

She thought about asking for the chocolate, then ate a few bites of the strawberry before pushing away from the table and standing up.

How were they going to handle the fact that she had no idea where to find her room—even though she'd supposedly been here long enough to know?

One of the guards solved the problem. "I'll go up with you, he said."

She nodded, letting him lead her up a broad flight of stairs to the second floor, then down a hall to room seven.

She tried to remember. Was seven a lucky number? Or was it just the opposite.

When she stepped inside, she heard the door click behind her. She was locked in, but she was finally alone, feeling like she'd been drifting through a waking dream. She turned the knob to check, but the door was definitely locked.

Looking up, she surveyed the room. It was pretty plain with a narrow bed, shelves along one wall and no rug or other decorative touches.

Quickly she crossed to the far side and stepped out onto a small balcony, breathing in the scent of a pine forest. The balcony might have been an escape route except that it was enclosed with a cage of mesh, the openings about the size of chicken wire. When she slipped her fingers through some of the spaces and pulled, it didn't move. Obviously it was stronger than chicken wire. Could she somehow get the mesh loose from the balcony railing? And if she'd been here for three weeks, wouldn't she have tried?

Leaning her head against the mesh, she closed her eyes, trying to clear her head. But it felt muzzier than when she'd first woken up—and the terrible thought skittered through her brain that there had been some kind of drug in her dinner.

She pulled at the mesh, forcing herself not to scream and not to sob. Probably they'd know it if she broke down, and maybe they'd come running in here to take advantage of her weakness.

Teeth clenched, she closed her eyes for a moment.

Either she was crazy, or Dr. Raymond and the rest of the people here were trying to convince her that she was.

She wanted to believe it was the latter, for all the good that did her. The one thing she knew for sure was that if she stayed here for long, she would never be the same again.

CHAPTER SEVEN

The wolf had stopped to take down a buck and eat some of the meat, reveling in the wild song coursing through his veins.

He could do this only occasionally where he lived. If anyone found a half chewed deer, they'd start hunting the creature that had done it. Always he'd come back later in human form to remove the evidence. Here he could get away with a wolf's normal hunting instincts.

He drank at a small, quick-flowing stream, the cold water a jolt to his system. Then, just for fun, he stopped to watch a couple of raccoons fishing. But he grew restless and pressed on, walking in the same direction, as though some invisible string were pulling him forward—dictating the exact direction he took.

Not long after he'd washed the blood from his mouth and face, he saw a building in the distance and knew it was his destination.

It was a massive house, out of place in the wilderness. Who had put it here? And why? Was it on national forest land, or did their property adjoin the park?

A warning flashed deep in his brain. This was the place that had drawn him, but he should turn around and get the hell away—before it was too late.

He dismissed that option with a snarl and crept closer, his wary gaze flicking from his surroundings to the house and back again. He saw the structure had two floors and several wings. It was built in a modern style, as though huge, rectangular modules had been trucked in and bolted together. Trees had been cleared around the foundations to make a perimeter, and a chain-link fence topped by razor wire enclosed the whole property. As he circled around, staying in the shadow of the trees, he saw that there was only one way in or out—a wide gate that faced the front of the building.

When a door opened and two men came out, he faded back into the woods far enough to hide his presence but still close enough to let him eavesdrop. Both men were muscular, rough looking types that Brand would categorize as security or bodyguards. Both were dressed in jeans and dark polo shirts, with light jackets, which would hide the weapons they were certainly carrying.

They stood on a small porch, where both of them got out cigarettes, lighting up and taking long drags of smoke into their lungs.

The wolf grimaced, fighting not to cough as the fumes drifted toward him. Cigarette smoke always played havoc with his lungs, and the deep woods were the last place he'd expect to smell it.

"How is it going?" one of them asked.

"Hard to tell," the other answered dismissively "She just got here, but I think we have her tied up in knots. I meant figuratively. She's free to walk around, at least on a limited basis."

"She's at dinner? With the ringers?"

"She finished, and I took her up."

"She ate enough to get her happy juice?"

"I couldn't tell."

"Is it going to make her spill her guts to Raymond?"

"Who knows? It's a pretty weird way to work. They should just torture the information out of her and be done with it."

"She might lie. And after that, they have a battered body to explain. This way they've got more options."

"I thought she was just gonna disappear when they're finished with her."

"Still, it's better not to have evidence of torture if someone stumbles over the body."

The wolf listened to the casual talk of torture and murder. Jesus, what was going on in this place?

They were talking about a woman they were holding here. They wanted information from her. And it sounded like she was in big trouble whether she told them or not.

He moved away from the men, wondering if there was a way to get onto the property. After turning a corner, he chanced getting closer to the fence and found a place where runoff had washed away the soil under the chain-link fence. He was thinking about digging out more of the soil and slipping under when he saw a man dressed liked the two he'd seen earlier walking along the edge of the enclosure, obviously doing a perimeter check. Were they expecting some kind of rescue operation, or was the patrol just a precaution? And how often did they come along?

Staying in the shadows, Brand kept circling the property, seeing that several of the rooms had sliding glass doors that opened onto small balconies. Two of them were entirely open, but one was caged like an enclosure for a dangerous animal at a zoo.

As he drew closer, he saw the woman they must have been talking about. She stood with her fingers thrusting through some of the holes in the mesh and her forehead pressed against the barrier.

While he watched, she straightened, and he saw a determination come into her face and body. She might be a captive, but she wasn't going to roll over and let these bastards grind their boots into her.

He felt a jolt of admiration—and more—as he took in her blond hair, her delicate features, and the small hands that clutched the mesh of her cage.

She looked beautiful, so vulnerable, and so desirable that he felt his heart squeeze inside his chest. Although the notion might be fanciful, he was sure the promise of meeting her was what had brought him to this place. More than that, he knew he had to rescue her—and make love with her.

Some part of his mind recoiled at the out-of-kilter reaction—and he scrambled for an explanation. Was she a witch? Was that why they were holding her here? Did she have some special power that affected men? Or was the burning attraction he felt reserved for him alone?

There were only questions—no answers. And as he slipped from tree to tree, she raised her head. Although the men had not spotted him, she easily found him in the shadows.

Their eyes locked, and they stared at each other for long moments. He had no idea what she felt, but he was seized by a jolt of sensation that made the fur on his body quiver.

And suddenly something like the fight or flight imperative kicked in. He had been a fool to come here. Now he should run from her before it was too late. No, it was already too late. The ability to flee was only an illusion. He shook off that dark notion and moved closer, until only about thirty yards of space separated them.

She watched his progress, and when he halted near the fence, disappointment flooded her face.

"Help me," she whispered. The plea might have been too low for a human to hear, but not for a wolf.

He nodded, every instinct urging him to dig his way under the barrier. But then what?

He was a covert operative, carefully trained by Frank Decorah and his agents. On a rational level, he knew what he should do if he wanted to help this woman. He should return to his camp, make some preparations, and come back tomorrow when he had a better idea of what he was doing. Teeth gritted, he turned and faded back into the woods, heading for his camp, making plans as he moved silently through the forest.

CHAPTER EIGHT

Brand made it a few hundred yards into the woods, every cell in his body screaming for him to turn around.

And finally the thought of leaving the woman caged and in danger made him almost physically ill. He turned and started back— an image blazing in his brain.

It was of himself, rushing the fence and slamming against it. He ached to find the men who had been talking about her and rip out their throats for what they had done to her—and their casual discussion of her situation.

And if he did any of that, he'd be shot as a rabid beast.

He came silently back, and he saw the woman still on the balcony behind the wire mesh. Now she was standing with her head bowed, her shoulders slumped in defeat.

The sight of her helplessness was like a knife twisting in his gut.

He made a small yipping sound.

Immediately, she raised her head, making eye contact again, their gazes locking.

"I thought you'd left me, but you came back," she breathed.

He nodded.

"You understand me?"

Unable to help himself, he nodded again, then sat and raised his paw in a silent salute.

37

As he did, she flattened her hand against the mesh, pressing her palm into the hard metal.

"My name is Tory," she murmured. "Please, I'm in trouble. Can you help me?"

The only thing he could do was nod. She had told him her name, and knowing it was a joy.

He wanted to tell her who he was, but there was no way for a wolf to speak. When he was on an assignment in animal form, he could use hand—or rather paw—signals. But she wouldn't understand them.

He scratched at the ground—the signal for staying—longing to make her understand that he wasn't leaving. But for now, his only option was to back away, his breath freezing in his lungs as he watched the way the hope in her eyes dimmed. Turning, she went back inside.

But he wasn't going to simply leave her here. He was sure he could get into the compound. Finding her would be more difficult—although he knew she was on the second floor and on which side of the house.

When a light went on in the room beyond the balcony, it was like a signal to him.

From the outside, he could see her room, which might not help him once he got into the building. He studied the layout as he walked along the fence, coming back to the place where he knew a wolf could slip under.

He sat down in the shadows, waiting with his heart pounding for the guard to return.

Now he silently counted, judging the time passing. He thought it was twenty minutes before the man came back, walking along the inside of the fence. The wolf growled deep in his throat and waited until the enemy was out of sight. Then he slunk to the barrier and enlarged the hole with his claws until there was enough room to wiggle under. Once on the other side, he scratched at the dirt again, making the hole smaller and pawing leaves over the ground to make it look like the rest of the surroundings.

Satisfied that his escape route was secure, he sprinted to the side of the house and moved around it, making sure he hadn't been spotted as he searched for a way in.

From inside her room, Tory stared at the spot where the wolf—or perhaps it was a big dog—had faded into the shadows under the trees, she fought the sensation that he was abandoning her.

But what would that mean? He was only an animal out on the prowl. Only an animal? Well, he seemed to be trained. The look in his eyes had been highly intelligent, and he'd nodded at her and raised his paw when she'd spoken to him. It was almost like he understood perfectly what she was saying and wanted to give her his name the way she'd told him hers.

She tried to shake the muzzy feeling from her brain. Had she really gone so far into wishful thinking that she was imagining that a wolf had understood she was in trouble and was coming in here to rescue her?

With a deep sigh, she lifted her hand up and scrubbed it over her face, trying to clear her thoughts. But they were so foggy that she wasn't sure that what she had seen was real— or if she'd imagined the whole thing. Did she think the wolf was her only real friend when everybody else was playing a role? And he was going to somehow get her out of this mess?

The thought brought a hollow laugh.

She took one more look into the darkness outside the asylum.

"Come back," she called.

There was no answer, and finally she switched on the overhead light and looked around her prison. Dr. Son of a Bitch had told her she'd been here for weeks, but there was nothing familiar about the room.

Silently she looked for something she recognized, once again examining the single bed along one wall and the shelves with folded clothing neatly lined up. She'd seen them a few minutes ago, but she couldn't remember them from before. In the bathroom she found a plastic cup, a toothbrush, a small bar of soap that looked like it had been used several times, and a box of tissues on the toilet tank. Of course there was nothing she could use to help her escape.

A memory flickered in her mind, and she touched the side of her face. One of the goons had smacked her at the airport, and she thought the spot still felt a little tender. Or maybe she was making that up to fuel her conviction that she'd just gotten here. Too bad she hadn't torn a nail trying to fight him off. Then she'd have proof of her conviction that she hadn't been here for weeks.

She felt grimy, but she didn't want to get undressed and take a shower, not when she wasn't quite steady on her feet and when she didn't know who might come in. She settled for washing her face and brushing her teeth before returning to the bedroom.

Kicking off her shoes, she flopped down on the mattress, not bothering to change her clothes or slip under the covers. It was in defiance of her normal behavior. Would the bastards that ran this place mark that up against her?

Patient refuses to wear nightclothes?

Lying in the dark, she listened for sounds around her. She heard nothing except perhaps the murmur of distant voices drifting up from the lower floor.

So were they all downstairs plotting their next moves against her? Or were they really watching *The Sound of Music*, and she was only being paranoid?

Trying to think logically made her head hurt, and she closed her eyes, gripping the side of the bed to steady herself. In her mind she was picturing someone coming to check on her.

If they did, she could pretend to be sleeping, then overpower him and get away.

The pipe dream was comforting. But she was pretty sure no one would give her a chance to escape—not after she'd almost gotten away at the airport yesterday.

Yesterday. She knew damn well it had only been the day before, no matter what everyone was insisting. She hung on to that conviction, even when her thoughts began to fuzz over as though mold spores were growing on them.

The wolf circled the house, staying close to the foundation, looking up for cameras recording his movements. As far as he could tell, there were none. The lack of video surveillance spoke of supreme confidence. Whoever had equipped this place was sure that nobody was coming to rescue the woman. Probably because nobody even knew where she was.

Brand halted as he heard the low buzz of voices inside, but the window was closed and he couldn't distinguish what anyone was saying. Even with his wolf senses, he could tell only that several different people were involved. He stopped to evaluate. One man was doing most of the talking. The others were listening and sometimes commenting.

Padding on, he came to an open door and felt a surge of excitement. It was an invitation into the building—or a trap. Yet he couldn't turn away.

Creeping cautiously closer, he was able to look into a kitchen, where a man wearing jeans, a knit shirt and a white apron was standing beside a sink, loading a dishwasher. No one else was in sight, and when the guy was finished he took off the apron, folded it over the back of a chair, and disappeared through a doorway.

Now or never, Brand thought as he slipped inside, paused to make sure he wasn't being observed, then sprinted across the kitchen to a darkened hallway, where he stood listening.

He could see a lighted room down the hall. It must have been the room where the people were talking. He could still hear their voices, and then a man stepped into the hall and headed in his direction. In the shadows, Brand froze, readying himself to turn tail and run—an animal that had somehow come in through an open door. Before spotting the wolf, the man stepped into a room along the hallway.

A bathroom Brand figured, as he heard what must be a stream of piss hitting a toilet bowl.

Silently he backed away. If he didn't want to be discovered, he'd better avoid the rest of the crew down the hall.

After turning in the other direction, he came to a broad flight of stairs leading up. He took them, coming out on a second floor landing, where he could look over the railing. Quickly he made his way along the hall until he came to a turn that cut off the view from downstairs. He hadn't been sure how he was going to proceed. But he knew a wolf had limitations in this situation. The animal had gotten him in, but he couldn't, for example, open a door.

He dragged in a breath and let it out. Taking a chance, he began to say the words of transformation in his mind. He pushed through it, muscles, skin and internal organs changing as he changed from wolf to man. Moments later, he was human again—also naked and vulnerable.

Hoping he wasn't going to run into anyone up here, he started opening doors, looking for clothing. The first rooms he came to were entirely empty. On the fourth try, he found a room with a bed along one wall and shelves holding clothing opposite it. Unfortunately, the clothing was for a woman, but he'd seen more guys here than women.

Two doors down, he found men's clothing that was about his size. He pulled on a pair of jeans and one of the knit shirts that he'd seen the guards wearing as they stood on the porch smoking.

The shoes were way too small. He left them where he found them, hoping he wasn't going to have to explain why he was barefoot.

Continuing down the hall, he tried the knob on each room. A few held beds and shelves like the ones where he'd taken the clothing. Some were empty. Ten rooms contained clothing—which gave him an idea of how many people were in the house, at least the ones who slept upstairs. One room had more shelves with bed linens and towels.

He crossed the balcony area, then came back to a room halfway down the hall where the door was secured with a heavy bolt.

One locked door up here. On the side of the house where he'd seen Tory.

It could be where they stored the drugs, but he didn't think so. This looked like a device designed to keep someone in—not out. He went back in the other direction, still seeing nothing similar on any other door.

He swallowed hard, then shot the bolt as quietly as possible, waiting the see if a guard came running. When no one appeared in the hall, he stepped inside, closing the door behind himself as he looked around. Deliberately ignoring the blond-haired woman lying on the bed, he checked the surroundings. He already knew that the sliding glass doors led to the totally enclosed balcony. Another door led to a bathroom, but the window was also secured by heavy screening bolted to the exterior wall. The window was large enough to climb through if the barrier were removed, but when he looked out, he saw a two-story drop to the ground.

Stepping back into the bedroom, he finally allowed himself to focus on the woman lying in the narrow bed.

Tory.

The first thing he saw was that she hadn't bothered to get undressed or climb under the cover.

She lay with her eyes closed, unmoving. Did the rhythm of her breathing denote sleep? Or was she faking it?

As he walked closer, his gaze swept her delicate face and the blond hair framing it.

He breathed in her scent, a mixture of soap and woman that should have been ordinary, but he found it intoxicating. His eyes skimmed over her body as he focused on the swell of her breasts, the slight curve of her hips under the sweatpants, the long legs and the graceful, long-fingered hands that lay at her sides.

As he took her in, his brain buzzed with raw emotions that he had never experienced before and couldn't name. A voice in his head urged him to turn and flee the room—flee whatever it was that drew him to this woman the way he'd been drawn to no other.

But the voice faded as he took a step closer, unable to turn away. He wanted to press his lips to hers, to undress her and draw her naked body against his, and he knew he was teetering on the edge of a journey from which there was no return.

Her features were relaxed, but as he leaned over her, he saw what looked like sleep change to determination.

The realization came too late as she lunged upward, trying to knock him aside.

CHAPTER NINE

Brand had quick reflexes, but he'd been completely wound up with his reaction to this woman. Her attack was so unexpected that he only dodged aside to avoid a direct blow to his face, even as he silently cursed his own stupidity.

He should have been prepared for her to react with hostility in this place where she thought everyone was an enemy.

Ducking low, he came down on top of her, pressing her arms to her sides, as he tried to keep her from doing him serious damage without hurting her. When she tried to ram him with her head, he reared back, almost getting a knee in the balls for his trouble.

The only way to subdue her without pounding on her was to get closer. He pressed his form to her, securing her with his weight and one arm while he tried to stop her struggling. But fear and determination kept her rolling from side to side, desperate to throw him off.

Even as he fought her, he felt himself reacting to the pressure of his body against hers.

"Don't. I'm not here to hurt you," he whispered.

She gave him a fierce look, and he knew she was preparing to redouble her efforts—until her gaze met his.

In one charged second she quieted. Still, he wasn't willing to trust her. She might be feigning acquiescence while preparing another assault.

"Your eyes ..." she murmured. "You have his eyes."

He didn't have to ask who she was talking about. His body went rigid as she delivered that bit of startling insight. Was that what his friends thought when they looked at the wolf?

"No," he denied.

"Did he send you?"

"Who?"

"The wolf."

He drew in a quick breath as he wondered how to answer. Finally, he settled on "Yes," because he couldn't explain the truth.

She relaxed under him, and he took a chance on rolling to the side. The bed was too narrow for him to put any distance between them, but at least he was no longer being driven crazy with the feel of her body under his.

"Did you come here to help me?" she asked, and the hope in her voice made his insides clench.

He had seen her outside, heard the men talking, and knew that she was in bad trouble. He could have told himself it was none of his business. Instead he'd found a way to get inside the building and into her room.

"Yes," he answered, vowing that he would make good on the promise.

She looked relieved before her expression turned wary.

"What?" he asked softy.

"Everybody here is ... an enemy."

"Yeah."

His agreement made her shiver.

"Are you real?" she asked as she turned on her side and studied his face. "Or did I make you up because I was longing for someone to get me out of this mess?"

Tentatively, she raised her hand, stroking the beard stubble on his cheek, then the line of his brows before lowering her hand to trace the shape of his mouth. Her touch was light, but it sent tongues of fire through him.

"Don't."

"You feel real," she murmured, then leaned to touch her lips to his. It was a light touch, but rich with sensuality. When she pressed more firmly, heat spread through his body. She had started the kiss. He could have pulled away. Instead he angled his head for better access, drinking in the taste of her. She opened for him, inviting more, and he was helpless to resist, his arms gathering her close as he swept his tongue along the inside of her lips, then the ridges of her teeth, drawing a moan from her as he deepened the kiss.

The way she responded to him was like a jolt of lightning sizzling through his body, arrowing downward to lodge in his cock. This was the woman he had craved all his life, only he hadn't realized that he was searching for her. It was easy to picture himself stripping off her clothes and pressing her naked body to his. He might have done it if an owl hadn't hooted outside, breaking the spell and reminding him where they were—and why.

Christ, what was he thinking? Suppose he'd allowed himself to get lost in the pleasure of making love with her, and someone came in? Yeah, that would be perfect.

He struggled to hold his emotions in check as he rolled away.

When she reached for him and tried to pull him back, he shook his head.

"We can't," he said in a gritty voice.

"I ... want ..."

"You want to forget where you are," he finished for her.

"Yes, but it's not just that," she answered.

"What if someone came in?"

She considered that, pressing a hand to her forehead. "I'm sorry. When you ..." She stopped and started again. "I'm too out of it to think straight. I don't even know your name, and look what we're doing."

"I'm Brand."

"That's your last name?"

"No, my first."

"No last name?"

"Probably better—for now."

"I'm Tory Robinson. No reason I shouldn't tell you." She made a small sound. "I have nothing to hide—from you, or anyone else as it turns out."

"Tory," he said softly, just to try out the syllable on his lips.

Her eyes turned pleading. "What's wrong with me? Nothing feels normal."

"I heard two guys talking out on the back porch. I think they drugged your dinner."

She thought about that for several moments.

"Yes, but not only then. They put me out on the way up here. Then when I tried to escape at the airport. Dr. Son of a Bitch was waiting for me in the car when the goons brought me back, and he gave me a shot of something that knocked me out again."

"Dr. Son of a Bitch?"

"Dr. Raymond." she answered in a shaky voice. "That's what I call him."

"He's running this place?"

She closed her hand around his arm. "You don't know? Then what are you doing here—dressed like one of them?" she demanded.

"I found the clothes in a room down the hall. I don't know much—except that your balcony puts you in a cage, and two guys were on the porch talking about getting information out of you."

"Yes." She swallowed hard, then went on rapidly. "As far as I can figure out, they're trying to drive me crazy."

"How?"

"Starting with the timeline. I'm pretty sure I was in New York City last night, but Raymond is trying to convince me that I've been here for weeks."

"What is this place?"

48

She considered the question for a few moments. "I guess it's supposed to be a private sanatorium, but if I had to guess, I'd say I'm the only real inmate here. The other patients are props to help work me over, so to speak."

"Why?"

Her expression hardened. "Raymond thinks I have some information he wants."

Brand tried to take it in, but the explanation was confusing. If he were objective, he might come to the conclusion that this woman really *was* nuts, except that in his gut he didn't think so.

On the other hand, they'd only been talking for a few minutes, and his impression of her was clouded by lust. All of which meant that he couldn't be sure that her version of reality was the correct one.

She could be locked in because she really was insane—maybe criminally insane. But in any case, he'd better keep one ear tuned to the door.

She'd closed her eyes.

"Tory?"

Her lids blinked open. "Sorry, I have to focus really hard to stay awake."

"Yeah. Can you tell me why you're here? What did you do?"

"I'm a dancer," she answered, then laughed softly. "I guess that's not really what you're after."

"Right."

"I'm featured at the Midnight Club in New York. Or I was," she added, despair creeping into her voice. "And I got mixed up with the wrong man."

The words hit him with the force of cannonballs. She'd been with a man, when she was his?

The thought came at him like a blow to the chest. He'd known her for only a few minutes, and she was his?

Then he ordered himself to pull back. Never mind his own explosive reaction; she was talking about a time before he even knew she existed.

Well, somehow he'd known she existed, waiting for him to come here. The thought was hardly logical, but he knew it was true.

"What man?" he asked, struggling to keep a note of accusation out of his voice.

"Johnny Denato."

"The Mafia guy?"

"Is he?"

"From what I've read in the papers," he answered, not willing to tell her that the security operatives at Decorah kept up with the goings-on in the underworld. It might help her to know his profession, but if she was somehow questioned about her visitor, the less she knew the better.

She was silent for several moments, and it looked like she was drifting off into space.

"Tory?"

She focused on him. "Sorry."

"It's okay. It sounds like they pumped a lot of stuff into you."

"Yes."

"You were telling me about Denato."

"Right. He came into the club and saw the show, and it seemed like he was interested in me. He asked me to dinner, and I was afraid to tell him I couldn't go with him. I mean, I knew my manager wouldn't like me turning down a good customer. Denato and I saw each other after the show a couple of times."

His whole body tensed as he waited for her to talk about a sexual relationship.

Instead, she said, "I kept waiting for him to pounce on me, but he was always a perfect gentleman. I started thinking he was going out with me for the wrong reasons."

"Like what?"

"Like he wanted people to see me with him—but he didn't really want to do anything ... sexual."

"Then why continue seeing you?" he asked, unable to keep the harshness out of his tone.

"Maybe he's gay. Maybe he wanted people to see him with a beautiful dancer."

That was one explanation that could make sense. Like that gay guy in The Sopranos who had to pretend he was straight. And when he finally let the others know the truth, they killed him.

She began speaking again. "He took me back to his apartment last night. It was the first time I'd been there. Or maybe it wasn't last night. Maybe they're telling the truth—it was weeks ago, and I've been in a fog ever since." Before he could comment, she hurried on. "And now the worst part. I was in the living room, and he had stepped into the hall to take a call. Men came in ... and killed him."

Brand blinked. "Say what?"

"He was murdered. I heard the shots. Then I saw him lying in a pool of blood in the foyer."

"And you called the authorities?"

Self-accusation filled her voice. "I should have, but I wasn't exactly rational. I decided I had to get out of his apartment—and out of town. I thought the cops would assume I was involved. And the murders would find out who I was and think I'd seen them, which I didn't," she added quickly. "I was afraid they'd kill me, too. I rushed back home. Then I realized I had to call the police. But it was already too late. Two guys arrive at my door a few minutes later."

She heaved in a breath and let it out before continuing. "I got out my apartment window, but they caught me and slapped something over my face, and I woke up in a small plane. On the way here." She sounded like she was fixing the details in her mind, as though she wasn't quite sure of exactly what had happened.

He stroked his hand up and down her arm, trying to imagine the whole scenario from her point of view. It had to be terrifying.

She gave him a questioning look. "I don't even know where we are."

"Upstate New York."

"Okay."

She rushed through the rest of the story. "Right before dinner I woke up in a chair in Raymond's office, like we'd been in the middle of a therapy session and I'd nodded off. That's when he claimed I'd been here for weeks. Outside in the sitting room, a woman named June was waiting for me. She said we had gotten to be friends, and it was time for dinner. I started feeling muzzy again as soon as I ate."

Brand cursed under his breath. It could be all made up, but he didn't think so. The story was too crazy for her to have invented it on the spot—and too detailed. "I'm sorry."

"Not your fault—unless they sent you in here to get me to cooperate. I meant like June—trying to convince me we're friends."

The despair in her voice was like a knife blade slicing at his soul.

He cupped his hands around her shoulders. "Look at me."

When she did, he went on, "I'm not like June." He said it softly, but he tried to project every ounce of sincerity he could muster.

She searched his face. "I want to believe you. Maybe that's a mistake."

"No."

"You could prove it by helping me get out of here."

He gave the only answer he could. "I want to, but I can't do it tonight."

Panic and disappointment claimed her expression. "Oh Christ. The longer I stay here, the more likely it is that he'll turn my brain to cottage cheese. I mean—with his drugs and the games he's playing."

The way she said it made his stomach clench. "No he won't. You're stronger than he is."

"How do you know?"

"You already tried to escape twice, and you attacked me when I came in here."

She winced.

"You aren't giving in. You were fighting him, even when you didn't know what you were up against." He dragged in a breath and let it out. "But I can't get you out of here tonight."

"Why not?"

"Because I'm not prepared. I stumbled on this place by accident, and I didn't bring any equipment with me. We have to do it tomorrow night."

"Fate brought you here to me."

He'd been thinking something similar. Fate or the ancient gods who had turned the males in his family into more than men.

"I know it's hard, but try to stay cool for a little while longer. Don't act like you're fighting the doctor. Pretend you're cooperating with him."

"Okay."

"I'll be back for you tomorrow. I promise."

She slung her arms around his neck and hung on tight, and he felt her tension, sensing that she was fighting not to sob.

"I know," he whispered.

"You can't know."

"I can understand desperation."

He ran his hands up and down her back, teetering on the brink, knowing that if he didn't get away now, he'd do something he'd regret.

Before he could change his mind, he stood up quickly and walked to the door.

CHAPTER TEN

Brand pressed his ear to the door and listened. When he heard nothing, he stepped into the hall, knowing that if he looked back at Tory again, he could never leave. But if he tried to spring her now, he could get her killed. That thought was the only thing that could make him keep his resolve.

As he stood in the hallway, the idea of locking her in again made him almost physically sick, but he had to do it. Everything had to be just as he'd found it.

He had just finished when he heard footsteps coming from the direction of the stairs.

He sprinted in the other direction, slipping into one of the empty rooms. The steps stopped at Tory's door, and he knew he had been just in time.

Holding the door open a crack, he looked into the hall.

A slimly built older man was looking around, his expression suspicious, and Brand suspected he might have heard someone up here.

Brand tensed, ready to flatten the guy if he came into the room where he was hiding.

To his relief, the man stayed where he was and tried the lock on Tory's door, then looked through a peephole at her.

Was it Dr. Raymond or someone else?

The man stayed where he was for long moments. Then he finally turned and left.

Brand waited for several minutes before checking the hall again and making sure it was empty. He didn't know the time, but he was hoping that a lot of the people here would already have turned in. Or maybe they were relaxing in front of a television set in some common room.

That still left him to decide how to get away. He'd come in as a wolf, and only a wolf could slip back under the fence. But was it better to stay as he was before he got there?

He stepped back into the room where he'd hidden and crossed to the window. When he looked out, he saw that it had the same view as Tory's. From here there was no good way down, but to his right, he saw the roof of the back porch where the kitchen door was located. From there, he could lower himself to the ground.

He was cautious as he stepped into the hall, then proceeded in the direction of the next room. Once inside, he closed the door behind him and crossed to the balcony, then quietly opened the window and scanned the grounds for signs of movement. This would be when he most visible if a passing guard happened to look up. Brand waited to be sure nobody had spotted him before easing the window up and stepping over the sill, coming down on the flat roof but staying low.

Again he listened and swept his gaze over the grounds around the house before crossing the porch roof and climbing over the edge, stretching out his arms to lessen the distance he would have to drop.

He hit the ground, stayed on his feet, and dashed to the side of the house where there were no doors. Pressed against the wood siding between two windows, he looked and listened for several moments. When he was sure he was alone, he began to unbutton his borrowed shirt. Next he pulled off his pants and balled up the clothing. Naked in the cooling spring air, he began to say the chant that would turn him into his more primitive persona. It was painful to keep changing form so often, but he saw no other alternative. It was one thing for a wolf or a big dog to be seen inside the fence. It was quite another for a strange man to get caught in here.

And it was the right choice to have made. Almost as soon as Brand had transformed, one of the guards came around the side of the house and stopped short when he saw the animal.

"What the hell?"

In one smooth motion, the man reached for the gun he carried in a holster at his side, unsnapping the shield and drawing the weapon. But Brand was already leaping forward, knocking the gun out of his hand and slamming the guard to the ground. Trying not to cause too much damage, he chomped down on the guy's gun hand. The man screamed, and Brand silently cursed. Knowing he had very little time now, he abandoned the pile of clothing he'd discarded and pelted for the fence.

He could hear loud voices behind him as he hightailed it toward safety.

"Patrick? What happened?" one of them asked.

"A wolf or a big dog attacked me."

"Jesus. Are you sure?"

"Yeah."

"How did it get in here?"

The man answered with an angry retort. "Who the hell knows?"

At the barrier, Brand scraped away the dirt he had kicked into place, then squeezed under the chain links, tearing the skin of his back as he forced himself through.

The guys must have stopped arguing about what had happened, because a shot hit the ground behind him as he sprinted for the woods. Behind him, lights snapped on, and a siren began to wail.

More shots followed him, but he was in the trees now, and he didn't think the men were coming through the gate to chase an animal—unless it had killed someone, which he'd been careful not to do. Still, he was remaking his plans as he put distance between himself and the compound.

An animal had gotten in. The guards would plug up the hole, and they'd be on the alert for intruders, which meant he'd need a wire cutter. And he'd have to proceed with extra caution when he came back tomorrow night.

Would they move Tory? The question made his throat clench. He'd counted on knowing where she was.

For a split second, he thought about contacting Decorah Security and asking for help. Then he thought about Tory's situation. He'd heard the men saying she was expendable. Would Dr. Son of a Bitch kill her if he thought she was going to be captured?

That danger meant stealth was Brand's best bet now. After he got her out of there, he could call for backup.

As footsteps pounded up the stairs, Tory forced herself to lie in bed with her eyes closed. She'd heard a shot, then lights had snapped on, and a siren began to sound.

Oh Lord, they must have spotted Brand.

But she was supposed to be drugged, and she couldn't react like a normal person would.

She lay rigid, her heart drumming inside her chest. In the next second, the door burst open, and Dr. Raymond charged in.

Her eyes blinked open, like she'd been sleeping.

"What?" she said in a quavery voice.

"Are you all right?" he asked as he looked around the room like he expected to find someone in here with her.

She'd wanted Brand to stay with her. Now she thanked God that he had left in time. But where was he? Was he all right?

"Yes," she managed to answer.

After a long moment, the doctor backed away, closed the door behind himself and locked it.

She lay with her heart still thumping, not knowing the outcome of the emergency. And not even sure what had happened. Her best guess was that someone had seen Brand—and shot at him. But had he gotten away?

Climbing out of bed, she crossed to the balcony and stepped out. In the light that now flooded the grounds, she could see men moving around the property, searching, and she had to conclude that if they'd found Brand, they wouldn't still be searching. They would already have hauled him inside for questioning—or killed him.

She shuddered. Now she had a better idea why leaving with Brand tonight would have been impossible.

She stood on the balcony for several more minutes, but the cool air finally forced her back inside.

Lying down again, she hugged her arms around her shoulders and rocked back and forth, praying that Brand was all right.

Although she'd never met him before tonight, she'd felt something for him that she couldn't even name. She'd started by wanting his help. But she wanted a lot more, too. She tried to analyze what she sensed about the two of them and finally concluded that it was a kind of instant recognition that they belonged together.

The thought startled her. Was it really true, or was that what her bombed-out brain wanted to believe?

It was true, she told herself. Or did she have to believe that because his leaving made her feel more alone than she ever had in her life? More alone than when she'd first come to this room.

And what about tomorrow?

She shuddered. The guards discovered an intruder inside the fence, and their defenses would be up.

Brand had said he was coming back for her, but what if that turned out to be impossible?

Teeth clenched, she ordered herself to stay calm because there was nothing else she could do.

Brand had woken her up from what she could only think of as a drugged sleep, and now the poison in her bloodstream was taking over again. She'd stayed as coherent as she could for him, but her mind was starting to feel like a flying circus, and she couldn't stop herself from wondering if she'd made up her late-night visitor.

Only, if she had, what about all the excitement outside?

She fought to stay awake, but the drugs in her system exerted a powerful draw on her. Her eyes flickered closed, and before long, she was sleeping.

And in sleep, she got what she wanted. A noise startled her, and she saw a shape in her room. At first she thought it was the animal she had seen earlier. Then she realized it was a man, walking purposefully toward her, his feet making no sound on the wooden floor. She couldn't see his face, and she knew she should be afraid. But fear wasn't part of the equation. She understood on some deep instinctive level that it was Brand coming back to help her make it through the night. Sitting up, she held out her arms to him.

When he'd been in her bed earlier, he'd kissed her and pulled her body against his, then told her they couldn't do anything else because he had to make sure no one came in and discovered them.

But this was different. They weren't in her room anymore. They were in a place where she didn't have to worry about Dr. Son of a Bitch charging in and seeing the man who was going to rescue her. She'd been lying on a hard, narrow cot. In this secret place, the bed was a lot wider and a lot cushier. And it wasn't in the place where she was being held captive. It was out in the middle of the forest, in a pretty little glen with a canopy of trees overhead and a carpet of bright green moss on the ground. The sweatpants and shirt she'd been wearing were gone, replaced by an almost transparent gown with a high waist and thin straps.

"I told you I'd come back," Brand said as he stood beside the bed.

"You didn't make me wait until tomorrow night. Thank you—for bringing me here."

"It wasn't me. You're the one who did it. You called me back," he said in a husky voice as he pulled the covers aside and slipped into bed with her.

His closeness made her heart leap.

"We both wanted to do more a little while ago," he said, then brushed his lips against hers.

It was a light kiss, his mouth only rubbing back and forth, demanding nothing she was unwilling to give.

His touch stirred her senses as no other man ever had.

Deep in her mind, she knew this time with him couldn't be real, but she pushed that notion aside because she didn't have to deal with reality—yet.

Although sensuality swirled inside her, there was still a little devil of doubt whispering in her ear.

You don't know him. Who is he really? What does he want from you?

She was sure he sensed her uncertainty. Lifting his head, he looked down at her.

"We don't have to do anything you don't want to do," he murmured. "Do you want me to leave you now?"

"No!" She heard the urgency in her own voice. "No. I need you with me."

"I'm here to please you."

He increased the erotic quality of the kiss, his lips moving over hers with an expertise that told her he knew how to pleasure a woman.

Mind and body, she responded to the sensuality of the encounter, craving more, craving everything he could give her.

And she sensed that he felt the same.

His tongue played with the seam of her lips, and she opened for him, wanting the kiss to deepen. He obliged her, turning his attention to the inside of her lips, then plunging farther in to stroke along the side of her tongue.

She made a small sound of protest when he withdrew—before he caught her lower lip between his teeth and gently nipped at her.

The protest turned to a purr.

"You like that."

"You know I do."

"And you don't want me to stop. Tell me what you want."

"Touch me."

"Like this?"

His fingers stroked her cheeks, her jawline, her neck, moving downward, sending tingles of sensation over her skin.

"Yes," she gasped.

"Where else should I touch you?"

"Don't make me tell you."

He laughed. "Then show me."

She tugged at the covers, dragging them down to her waist, showing him her body through the thin fabric of the gown.

His gaze was like an erotic touch as he focused on the hard points of her nipples. Reaching out, he circled one distended bud with his finger. She gasped as heat shot downward through her body to her core.

He watched her face as he played with both nipples through the gown.

Then he pulled the garment up and over her head.

He cupped her breasts, cradling them in his hands before his thumbs skimmed over the hardened tips again, sending another wave of sensation through her.

She brought her hands up to clasp his broad shoulders. They were bare. Had he been dressed when he'd walked toward her through the forest?

She couldn't remember. But now he was naked in her bed, offering her escape from captivity—the only escape she could hope for tonight.

She brought her lips back to his, kissing him with an intensity that bordered on desperation as he continued to play with her breasts, squeezing them, twisting and pulling on the nipples, making her arch toward him.

"Please."

"You need to come?"

"You know I do."

He eased her down, so that she lay beside him hot and at the same time, vulnerable.

"Open your legs for me."

She did as he asked,

His gaze burned into hers as he stroked one hand down her body, slipping into the warm, wet folds of her sex.

"You're so ready for me."

"Yes." She had never been more ready for sex.

He kept his gaze locked with hers as he began to stroke her there, dipping into her vagina, making her hips rise to meet his touch. The devilish finger moved upward, circling her clit, making it swell before he slid down to her vagina again, plunging in and out, and imitating the motions of intercourse.

When he pulled his hand away, she cried out.

"Don't stop."

"What do you want?"

"I want you inside me."

"We can't—not now."

"Why not?"

"You know why not. Because we have to wait until I get you out of the Refuge."

She fought to drive that reality out of her mind and focus on release.

He changed his position, moving between her legs and bending to bring his mouth down to her sex. At the same time, he eased two fingers into her, pumping them in and out as he licked and sucked at her clit.

Her hips rocked, moving with him, begging for completion. And finally she came in an explosion of pleasure that rocketed through her.

Moments later, her eyes flew open, and she gasped when she saw where she was—in the narrow bed, locked in a room from which there was no escape unless Brand came back for her.

Her hand was between her legs, and she pulled it away, then lay very still, her breath coming fast and hard.

She looked around, hoping she hadn't cried out in her sleep. She'd just had the most vivid sexual experience of her life, and it had been in a dream.

Her cheeks burned as she lay there in the dark, going back over the intimate encounter. She'd been shameless in her behavior. But it hadn't been real. You could be shameless in a dream, and nobody would ever know. And maybe she could blame it on the drugs. They must have done something to her, like swept away her inhibitions. That and the visit from Brand.

A horrible thought struck her. What if they had a camera in here and someone had been watching her pleasure herself? Then she told herself they didn't. If there was a camera, someone would have come running the minute Brand had stepped through the door.

She closed her eyes, trying to relax. Brand was coming back for her tomorrow. All she had to do was get through the next day with her sanity intact.

Right. Not a big task, but she knew it was going to be the most horrible day of her life—well, maybe the second most horrible—after seeing Johnny Denato lying in a pool of blood on the floor in his foyer.

CHAPTER ELEVEN

Alexander Raymond was pacing back and forth in his office when his head of security, Gene Costa came in.

The doctor deliberately sat down in the chair behind his desk before demanding, "What the hell is going on out there?"

He'd heard shots fired, but after checking on Tory, he'd gone back to his office to avoid getting hit by a stray bullet. When he'd taken this job, he had looked forward to the elaborate scenario that he'd set up. Unfortunately from the first, things hadn't gone exactly as he'd planned.

The little twit had escaped from the men who had brought her up from New York. Thank God the airport was enclosed so that she hadn't gotten very far. That was all he needed—failure before the project ever had a chance to succeed.

He was being paid very well for this job, and he saw it as a stepping stone in his reputation as a can-do mental health expert. Or rather a can-do mental health destroyer.

His head of security was about to give him a summary of the recent disturbance when there was another knock at the door.

He glanced at Costa, who shrugged.

"Come in," Raymond called, fighting to keep annoyance out of his voice.

He and the security chief turned to see Will Monroe, one of the grunts, standing in the doorway with what looked like a shirt and a pair of pants tucked under his arm.

"What's that?" Raymond demanded.

"We found a pile of clothing near the side of the house." He pulled the shirt and pants from under his arm and held them up. They were standard security staff issue.

Raymond's eyes narrowed as he stared at the clothing. "How did they get there?"

"We don't know."

"Are you saying one of the guys went out and took his clothes off? Is someone dipping into the drug supply?"

Monroe shrugged.

Raymond's gaze swung back to Costa. "Give me a timeline of what's happened this evening."

"One of the guys saw a big dog ..." he hesitated for a moment, "Or a wolf prowling around outside the fence. Then Patrick was outside when the animal attacked him."

Raymond kept his gaze on the man. "Attacked how?"

"Patrick saw the animal lurking near the house. He reached for his gun to take it down, but before he could shoot, it charged him and knocked the weapon out of his hand. Then it dashed for the fence. We followed it to the place where it squeezed under and escaped."

"Wait a minute—how could it squeeze under the fence?"

"It found a place where it could dig out a passageway in the dirt."

Raymond considered that. An animal had had the notion to crawl under a chain-link fence and come in here? But why?

"You're sure?" he asked, half wondering if the security staff had been drinking. No. They looked sober—and worried.

"It was in a tearing hurry when it left—literally," Costa was saying. We found some bloody skin and fur on the bottom metal prongs."

"And then what?"

"It escaped into the forest."

"Did anyone follow?"

"We were too busy securing the interior here. Plus, by the time we got out the gate, it would have been long gone."

"You should have asked for instructions," Raymond muttered, thinking that maybe he should have gone out to supervise.

"It was a judgment call."

"Next time, ask me how to proceed."

"Yes, sir."

He kept his gaze on the two security men. "And there was no indication that a human followed the animal onto the grounds?"

"No, sir," Costa answered. "We're positive about that."

"But someone could have sent the dog in to have a look around?"

"Yes sir," Costa answered, sounding just a little bit doubtful on the logic of that idea. Like, how could a dog make a report? Well, it could if it was equipped with a camera.

"I want patrols doubled until we figure out that nobody's coming in here. And I want you to peruse the woods to make sure that dog wasn't with a man."

"Should we wait until morning?" Costa asked.

"Have a quick look around now. Then go back as soon as the sun's up," he ordered.

"Yes, sir."

"And inform me at once if you find anything."

They talked for a few more minutes, but there was nothing else that Raymond could think of at the moment.

When they left, he crossed to the cabinet at the side of his office, opened the lower compartment and took out a bottle of Scotch. He never drank during the day, but there were times when he allowed himself to indulge in the evenings, and this was one of those times.

He poured out two fingers and sat down in one of the easy chairs, where he took a large swallow of the burning liquid as he thought about what had happened.

As he went back to the puzzle of the discarded clothing, several scenarios went through his mind. Like could some of the staff be gay—and they'd been interrupted during a tryst outside? Interrupted by a large dog. That seemed highly unlikely.

He set down his glass, crossed to his desk and picked up his laptop, which he brought back to the chair. Pulling up the wounded man's personnel file, he studied the information. Patrick had a spotless record. And all he'd done tonight was get attacked by an animal that wasn't supposed to be on the property.

What had the damn dog been doing in here, anyway? Why dig under a fence to get into a secure facility?

Raymond went back to the camera idea—which sounded pretty far-fetched. Still, there was no good explanation for what had happened.

Suppose a thief were interested in this upscale house out in the middle of nowhere? Or was there any way someone knew that Tory Robinson was being held here?

The theft part had merit. But how could anyone know Tory was here. Still, he'd better be prepared for anything. Too bad he'd been too sure of his security measures to install cameras. Could Costa do it? He'd have to ask if the security chief had the necessary training.

His gaze kept flicking to the phone on his desk, half expecting a call from Gary Freemont, the man who was paying big bucks for Raymond to interrogate the woman.

This was the biggest case he'd ever handled—and he'd come a long way since he'd practiced winding his parents around his little finger. He'd convinced them he was the kid in the family worth sending to college, and he'd never looked back.

An undergrad degree in psychology had helped his understanding of human nature tremendously. It really hadn't been necessary to waste any more time sitting in class rooms. He'd grown a small beard to make himself look older, faked his PhD credentials and gone on from there.

He took a sip of Scotch as he thought about the clever moves he'd made.

He'd started his alternate career as a staffer at a halfway house before moving on to Garfield State Hospital, then quit before the chief of staff figured out that he was trying some mind manipulation experiments on the patients. But he'd gotten a good handle on some effective techniques—like creating confusion about how long a person had been in treatment.

After leaving Garfield State, he'd gotten the backing of a private benefactor who had paid his salary at an upscale institution in the DC suburbs where some interesting political types had gone for secret treatment. His two years there had been a good education in how to twist the minds of people who thought they were above the law.

But he'd wanted a place where he was the one in charge. And he'd found this facility, which was isolated enough for him to do anything he wanted—like hiring staff that had no interest in the welfare of the inmates and creating a bogus patient population where the only real one was the person he'd been hired to break down.

It had worked well with half a dozen patients, including a mobster's wife who had tried to leave her husband. Before she'd gone, she'd raided his safe and taken cash and jewelry. She had been determined not to spill the whereabouts of the stash. Raymond had gotten her to talk—and conveyed the information to her husband. When the guy had given him the go-ahead, Raymond had put her out of her misery, then buried her in a pretty little grove of trees in the national forest.

That was his first murder. It had helped him solidify his well-earned reputation.

But this particular project seemed to have hit a snag. He had to find out what was going on—and cut off the interference before it could blossom into something a whole lot more serious.

Or before Gary Freemont found out about the clusterfuck that was going on up here.

But how would he—unless he had a spy on the staff?

"Now who's paranoid?" Raymond muttered.

He and Freemont had met through a satisfied customer, Ned Hermann. Raymond had just handled a delicate matter for the man, involving a whistleblower named Jeff Pareles.

Pareles had thought he had the evidence to send Hermann to jail for padding a government contract and pocketing the extra money. After Raymond had finished twisting his mind in knots, Pareles had ended up taking a nosedive off the top of the headquarters building, and Hermann had faked e-mails that made the whistleblower look like the guilty party.

Raymond had been flush with success, and he'd bragged that he could get anyone to do anything he wanted—up to and including shooting their grandmother. Now he wished he hadn't done such a good sales job. What if he couldn't deliver?

Freemont was a dangerous man—as dangerous as Johnny Denato. And he was going to expect results for his retainer.

Raymond realized he had clamped his hand around the glass of Scotch. Deliberately relaxing his grip, he told himself that he wasn't going to fail. Tory Robinson would tell him what he wanted to know, and Raymond would deliver the information to Freemont.

That is—if Tory *had* the information. Freemont had been sure she did. But what if he was wrong? Would that turn into a case of "shoot the messenger"?

Raymond swallowed the last of the Scotch in the glass, thinking he should have gotten better background information on the dancer's relationship with Denato before jumping into this deal. Next time, he'd be more careful about accepting an assignment.

Brand stayed in the shadows under the trees, watching men crisscross the property, running around like rabid dogs. He wanted to stay and watch. No, that was only part of the truth. He wanted to stay because Tory was in there, and the thought of leaving her in the clutches of those bastards made his throat clog. Every werewolf instinct urged him to rush back to defend her. But the human brain inside the animal's skull was better equipped to make decisions.

He knew he had to get back to his camp and make some plans. Too bad it was so far away. If he'd really known that he was coming to this place, he would have pitched his tent closer. On the other hand, if the camp were closer, the security staff might find it—and find him. Better to have some distance between them tonight.

Clouds had covered the moon, but he didn't need moonlight to see. He moved through the woods with a wolf's skill, all his senses sharp and probing. And always he was on the alert to make sure no man was following him. Earlier he'd taken a leisurely route, enjoying the forest and the hunt. This time he wanted to go directly back to his camp, but he forced himself to take a long detour through a stream, in case anyone was trying to follow him.

Then he was back on track, stopping just before he reached his tent, pausing in the shadows to make sure nobody was in the area before changing his form once more, wincing as the transformation hit the patch of skin that he'd torn as he'd wrenched himself under the fence. He pulled on his pants and carried his shirt inside. The change from wolf to man had made the wound bleed again. Getting out his first-aid kit, he put some antiseptic on the ripped places, then added a bandage which he could leave on only until his next change. But it would keep him from getting blood on his clothing.

After drinking from his water bottle, he lay down, thinking he would make plans for tomorrow. But the moment he got horizontal, he was transported back to the time when he'd been lying beside Tory in bed. He'd held her in his arms, kissed her, and longed to do a whole lot more. Now he felt his cock stiffen at the memory. It was tempting to go with the fantasy and take it to its logical conclusion. Instead he told himself he'd better focus on what he had to do tomorrow. It was too damn bad that the guard had stumbled on him inside the compound. Obviously the whole place was on alert now, and they were probably most interested in the spot where the large dog had clawed his way under the fence. The hole would be blocked up by now. And there would be extra patrols. But he'd have different considerations on his next visit. He'd tried to hide his presence because he couldn't get Tory out immediately. When he left again, she was going with him, and it didn't matter what he did to the guys who were in there guarding her.

He switched on his tablet and looked up Johnny Denato. The man was a big deal in the New York underworld, and Brand expected to see a detailed story about the murder in the New York Times. But there was nothing on the front page or any other page, as far as he could see.

It looked like someone had killed Denato and hushed it up—like it never even happened? Or what if everything Tory had told him was a lie? He didn't want to believe it, but he should do some checking.

After an internal debate, he called the Midnight Club and asked for Tory Robinson.

"Who wants her?" a gruff voice asked.

"A friend."

"Well, she didn't come in to work the last two nights, and she didn't bother to give us any warning. She left us in the lurch. If you see the bitch, tell her she's fired."

So she'd disappeared suddenly without giving notice. That squared with her story.

He wanted to ask if she'd been dating Johnny Denato, but he knew that was a bad idea. He was using his own phone. He didn't want anyone associating him with the gangster.

The guy hung up, and Brand thought Tory would have been a lot better off if she'd called the cops while she was still in Denato's apartment. But then Brand wouldn't have met her. And maybe the killers would have been able to eliminate their chief witness.

It was like the fates had conspired to put her smack in his path. But the circumstances were a lot less than ideal. No matter what was really going on, she was in bad trouble, and he had to snatch her away from a terrifying and dangerous situation.

Brand turned off the phone to keep from running down the battery.

He grabbed a notepad and pen and started making a list of things he was going to need tomorrow—starting with a wire cutter. He already had a knife, his gun, rope. Too bad a wolf backpack couldn't carry too much.

He'd have to bring only what was essential. Did he need clothing for Tory? Thinking back over their meeting, he remembered that she'd lain down on her bed fully dressed, and her shoes had been on the floor. That was good. He wouldn't need clothing for her, but he'd better bring some food.

He switched on the tablet again and called up a geologic survey map of the area, looking for the closest route to civilization. Then he studied satellite photos, trying to find landmarks that might help him.

He was as ready as he could be when he laid down—preparing for sleep. But even as he closed his eyes, his mind would not shut off.

He was almost thirty, the age for werewolf bonding, and he'd been certain that the need to find a mate was stirring painfully inside him.

He'd tried to ignore it, but he'd felt the pressure building. Now that urgency was gone. He felt calm. And it was because he'd met his mate.

Although he'd fought his destiny tooth and claw, the feeling of inevitability was like a balm, and he wondered why he had resisted it so assiduously.

Finally calm, he felt himself drifting off, and he was grateful for the respite because he knew that if he didn't get some sleep, he wouldn't be in good enough shape to get Tory out of there.

A disturbing thought prodded him like a sharp stick into his side. Last time, he'd come into the compound as a wolf, and it would be convenient if he had that option again. But he couldn't do it in front of Tory. She didn't know that the wolf she'd seen and the man were one and the same. He'd have to find the right time and the right way to tell her, and that didn't include a nasty surprise that would shock her to the core.

CHAPTER TWELVE

A persistent buzzing like an alarm clock that wasn't sure whether to go off or not woke Tory. It stopped, and she opened her eyes, looking around the unfamiliar room. For a frightening moment, she had no idea where she was. The fear expanded when it all came rushing back to her like a tidal wave ready to suck her out to sea. Finding Johnny Denato dead. Trying to get out of town. Being taken north and almost getting away.

She was a captive here, but Brand was coming for her today—if she hadn't made him up. No, he was real. She had to believe that. And she had to keep herself sane until he came back.

She hated the feeling that she needed him to rescue her. Yet that appeared to be her only real means of escape from a man who seemed bent on destroying her mind.

Clenching her fists, she struggled for calm. Dr. Raymond was real, but so was Brand. He *was not* a figment of her imagination, and he was coming back tonight.

A knock at the door made her jerk up.

The door opened, and a man with short blond hair stuck his head inside. "Breakfast in twenty minutes," he said, his tone upbeat. "I'll be back to collect you."

"Okay," she answered, waiting until he closed the door again before she got up and looked at the sunlight streaming through the sliding glass door. It was broken up by the pattern of the grating that enclosed the balcony.

She turned away and headed for the bathroom where she used the facilities, then gave herself a long look in the mirror as she brushed her teeth, thinking that she looked drawn and defeated. Probably that was what Dr. Son of a Bitch wanted, and the more she looked beaten, the better. All she had to do was get through today, she told herself, praying it was true. And if it was just today, maybe she could take chances that would be dangerous on a long-term basis.

With a vague plan forming in her mind, she turned toward the shower. She didn't really want to get undressed, but she did want to start off the day feeling fresh. Returning to the bedroom, she gathered a set of clean clothing and underwear and brought them into the bathroom, setting them on the edge of the sink while she took a hot shower. She wanted to stay under the spray for hours but got out after a few minutes, knowing she had a limited amount of time.

She dried off and dressed quickly, then looked for a hair dryer, which she didn't find. Interesting. Hadn't June said that Tory had complained about hers being broken? Maybe it still was. Or maybe there never had been one in here.

She towel-dried her hair, telling herself she wasn't going on stage at the Midnight Club.

That thought stopped her for a second—as she considered what her hair had looked like before she showered. Actually, the same as it had when she'd finished her last performance and gone out with Johnny Denato.

That was another clue to Dr. Son of a Bitch's veracity. He'd been so careful to build up a case for her having been here longer than overnight, but apparently coiffeurs were a detail he hadn't thought about. She'd put some darker streaks into her hair to try something different. But if she'd been here for weeks, the streaks would have grown out—or gotten dull.

Unless he'd touched up her hair himself, he was lying about the time frame. It also reminded her of something else. Drugs. He'd given her a shot that knocked her out at the airport. And she'd felt disoriented after dinner—probably from something in her food. She'd better not eat too much, or maybe there was some other way she could avoid the secret medication.

She was dressed when the guy came back for her. He brought her down to the same dining room where she'd had dinner with the other patients—if they really were patients.

She looked at each of them in turn.

June was the one who'd said they were friends. But would she really have been waiting for Tory to finish a session with the doctor?

The balding man who looked like he was in his sixties was Ted. The younger guy was Arthur. And the woman in her twenties was Robin.

They all nodded to her as she came into the dining room.

Tory looked to the sideboard and saw that plates of eggs, bacon, fruit and cinnamon buns were laid out like a buffet, along with various kinds if cereal and yogurt. Coffee and tea urns were on a serving cart. The arrangement was a relief, because everybody would be eating the same thing—which meant they couldn't be drugging her—unless they were drugging everybody.

She walked to the end of the line, watching Arthur take eggs, bacon, fruit and a bun. She made the same selections and noted what other people were taking. Everybody had bacon. June skipped the eggs and got a peach yogurt. Robin had two cinnamon buns.

"How did you sleep?" June asked as they sat down together along one side of the table.

"Okay—but something woke me up. Noise outside like firecrackers." She looked around. "Did anybody else hear it?"

Nobody else had. Were they lying? Or in denial?

Worry and uncertainty were still affecting Tory's appetite, but she tried to make herself eat a substantial meal, because it might be the only one today that wasn't tainted.

She was still eating when the guy who had escorted her to the dining room came back.

"Group therapy time," he announced.

Tory's stomach clenched, and she was afraid she was going to throw up the food she'd just swallowed.

She looked at June. "Group therapy?"

The other woman nodded and stood.

Tory wanted to cling to the edges of her chair, but everybody else was standing, and she got the feeling that if she didn't follow the crowd, she was going to end up being carried.

She let the group sweep her along to a room near Raymond's office. Comfortable chairs were arranged in a circle, and all of the patients sat down. She and June took seats next to each other with a small table in between. Nobody spoke as they waited, but Tory could sense a feeling of expectation buzzing in the room, like at a play when the audience was waiting for the curtain to go up.

Finally Dr. Raymond came through the door, looking all business. He was carrying a tablet and sat down in a chair at the head of the room.

"How is everyone this morning," he asked.

Everybody said that they were fine, which was really stupid. If they were mental patients, they obviously weren't fine.

"Is there anything you want to share?" he asked.

Tory decided to try the question she'd asked at breakfast. "I heard something outside last night."

"Yes?"

"It sounded like shots—or firecrackers. What happened?"

"I thought you were asleep when I came in to check on you," he shot back.

"Was I? I don't remember." She looked around at the rest of the people in the room. "You all said at breakfast that you hadn't heard anything."

The doctor pulled an annoyed face, like they'd given the wrong answer—or he had.

"Let's get down to business," he said, looking at Robin. "You shared with us that your father molested you from the time you were eight until you left for college. And that you'd repressed the memories—until you found that you were having trouble being intimate with anyone you met on campus."

Tory winced, and Raymond's gaze shot to her.

"That upsets you?"

"Of course. Wouldn't it upset anyone?"

The doctor looked around at the rest of the group. "Who else was upset?"

The others shifted in their seats. June raised her hand and put on a concerned face. The men looked like they could care less about what had happened to Robin. Which might just mean that they were too self-obsessed to care about anyone else.

"You were traumatized over time," the therapist said.

"Yes."

"But sometimes it only takes one incident to change the course of your life." He looked at Tory. "You haven't talked about witnessing Johnny Denato's murder."

She looked down at her hands, thinking that he'd finished with Robin's problem pretty fast. And would a therapist who cared about his patient really bring up something like that in a group session? Wouldn't he wait for the patient to make the first move when the subject was so sensitive? And was he saying that she'd been sitting here for weeks without opening up to the others? That didn't exactly make sense, either.

"I'd like you to tell us about the murder," he said.

She raised her head. "What if I don't want to?"

"I think it's time," he said.

"Well, I didn't see it."

"That contradicts the reports in the papers."

"It was in the papers?" she asked.

He smiled, a smile that made her wonder if he was lying. "Yes, you're quite famous."

She struggled not to react.

"Why don't you tell us what happened?"

"I was in his apartment," she said in a flat voice. "He got a phone call and went out into the foyer to take it. I heard voices. Then I heard shots. I got up and hid behind the drapes while the killers searched the apartment. After they left, I ran away."

"Oh, you poor thing," June said, patting her on the shoulder. "Thank you," Tory murmured, thinking that maybe she should string this out as long as she could. She might make Raymond mad, but so what? He wasn't going to kill her. He wanted information from her. At least that was what she was counting on.

"Why are you here?" she asked June.

The woman's gaze flicked to Raymond, and he gave an almost imperceptible shake of his head.

"We were talking about you," June said. "Now that you're finally told us about the murder, I hope you'll tell us the rest of the story."

Who were these people, Tory wondered. Had Raymond, if that was his name, gotten them from some acting company? Would actors have agreed to a nasty job like this? Or maybe they didn't know the truth about what was going on here. Maybe they all thought she was a criminal, and they were aiding the authorities.

The doctor was looking at Tory. "Go on," he said.

She licked her lips. "I made an error in judgment. I should have called 911 right then. But I was afraid, and I ran away."

"You were really going to call the cops?" Ted asked.

"Not at first. Then I knew I'd made a mistake. I should have called them right away."

79

"But weren't you having a sexual relationship with Denato?" he pressed.

"No," she shot back. "And what's that got to do with anything?"

Before Ted could respond, Raymond answered. "Your relationship with him is important. It's better not to lie about it. He had a reputation as a womanizer, and you were seeing him for several months."

"More like several weeks."

She saw Raymond react to her words and swung toward him.

"What?" she demanded.

"I was told you were with him longer than a few weeks. And that you got to know his men."

"I was never *with him*. I was only dating him casually. Who told you differently?"

"I'll ask the questions," he answered, punching out the statement, but she could tell that he was worried about her answer. Why was that important?

She looked around at the group. "You can believe what you like. And what would my relationship with Denato have to do with my staying or running away?"

"Maybe if you'd been close with him, you would have stayed," Arthur answered.

"Yeah, if I'd known him better, I might have felt an obligation to stick around."

The therapist shot Arthur an annoyed look.

Maybe because the man was on the spot, he came out with some more information. "The cops want you for questioning."

CHAPTER THIRTEEN

Tory felt her insides clench. But was that even true? Or was Arthur saying it for effect? It could be they didn't know for sure that she'd even been at the apartment. There was no way of knowing.

She raised her chin and asked in a voice that she hoped was steady, "How do you know I'm wanted for questioning?"

Panic flashed across Arthur's face. "Um—I heard people talking."

"What people?"

"The staff."

The doctor stepped in to cut off her interrogation of the other patient. "Let's not get off track. We're trying to help Tory get over a traumatic incident. She saw the killers, but she doesn't want to remember that."

She swung toward him. "I didn't see the killers! I was behind the curtains."

The doctor shook his head like he was sorry she couldn't allow herself to remember.

"And if I'm wanted for questioning, shouldn't I be in New York talking to the authorities?"

Raymond's gaze bore into Arthur, like the guy was an understudy in a performance, and he'd forgotten his lines.

The man's cheeks reddened, and Tory hoped he was going to get in trouble for leading them onto the wrong track.

Around the room, the other patients were shifting in their seats, waiting for a cue from the doctor, she assumed.

She kept her eyes on him, watching his face take on a decisive look. "I think it might be time for our mid-session snack."

He pressed a button on his phone, and one of the attendants came in, carrying a tray of glasses and a plate of cookies. Unless the cookies were in some particular order, they should be okay, Tory figured. But she saw the guy handing each of the patients a tall glass of what looked like orange juice.

He set June and Tory's drinks on the little table between them, each glass near one of them. June was reaching for hers, when Tory called out to the man who had brought the refreshments,

"Wait! Didn't you forgot the chocolate chips?"

The guy looked startled. "Was I supposed to bring chocolate chips?"

While everyone was focused on him, Tory glided her hand to the glass on June's side of the table and picked it up while pushing hers toward June. Apparently, June didn't notice the positions were switched. When Tory took a sip of her juice, June picked up her glass and did the same.

Tory watched her, thinking that if her drink was drugged, then the early part of the meeting was mostly for show, and now they'd be getting down to business, although Ted's annoyed observation didn't sound like it.

"You'd think they could have fresh orange juice," he complained.

"Why?" Tory asked, realizing that they were probably marking time until the drug began to work.

"This place is expensive," he answered.

"And who is paying my bills?" Tory asked, thinking that the more questions she could dredge up, the longer she could run out the clock. How long could this session last, anyway?

"You're here on a pro-bono basis."

"Why?"

"Because you were too messed up to function," the doctor answered in a sharp tone.

"What was I doing?"

Raymond looked around the room. "Do you really want me to talk about that in front of the others?"

"Yes."

"You were almost catatonic."

"Which means?" she asked.

"Completely unresponsive."

"And what snapped me out of that?"

"Drug therapy."

The others were sipping their juice. Tory had kept her tumbler clutched in her hand so that there could be no mix up with the one that June had. When she saw Raymond looking at her, she took another swallow, then another.

June did the same. After a few moments, she put her glass down with a clunk on the little table.

"I don't feel so well," she said in a shaky voice.

"Oh, what's wrong?" Tory asked, putting her hand on June's shoulder the way the other woman had done with her earlier.

"My head feels kind of muzzy."

Raymond looked from June to Tory and back again. "Could you have mixed up your glasses?" he asked, obviously struggling to keep his tone even.

"I don't think so," Tory said, as she took another sip of her drink. "And what would that matter anyway?"

"It wouldn't," the doctor snapped, still looking at her with suspicion. She'd bet he was angry, but he was fighting hard not to show it. Hopefully, she wrecked his plans for the next few hours.

Her thoughts were interrupted by a knock at the door.

"Come in," Raymond called, looking more annoyed than ever.

One of the tough-looking security men stepped into the room.

"Dr. Raymond, there's something you need to see."

"Right now?"

"Well, that would be best. Rain is in the forecast, and the tracks might be washed away."

"What tracks?" Tory asked.

"Nothing you need to worry about." The doctor got up and looked from Tory to June, who was slumped to the side in her chair. "We might as well end now, anyway."

The others stood up. June stayed where she was with her eyes closed and her hand gripping the arm of her chair.

"I'll stay with you in case you need anything," Tory said as the three other patients filed out of the room.

Her heart was pounding as she looked toward the open door. She was almost sure that Raymond and the other participants had been about to get down to the real work of the group, and it wasn't going to be pretty. As far as she could tell, Raymond thought she knew Denato's killers, and he was determined to get the information out of her. Only she didn't know.

Another thought struck her. What if Raymond was involved in the murder, and this charade was part of a cover-up?

She held back a moan, thinking that any way you sliced it, she was in a hell of a mess. But switching the glasses had given her a little reprieve.

And then one of the guards had come in all excited. She'd bet that had something to do with Brand's escape last night. Was there some way she could find out what was going on? And was the guard's summoning of Dr. Son of a Bitch going to mess up Brand's plans for tonight?

That thought was like a wave of ice water slamming her body.

* * *

84

Raymond followed Costa down the hall. "What is it? This better be good. You interrupted an important therapy session."

"You asked to be informed at once of any developments."

"Yes," he snapped, remember the meeting the previous night.

Still, he was annoyed as his mind clicked back to the therapy session. Probably it had been going to go nowhere because Tory had somehow switched drinks with June. Did that mean she suspected that her glass had a strong hallucinogen mixed in with the juice? Or had she simply grabbed the wrong glass?

He thought about how the little incident had gone down. No, he'd bet that Tory had directed everyone's attention toward the attendant, using that chocolate chip comment, then grabbed June's glass. Which would mean that she was still in full resistance mode. And he'd better get some damn results this afternoon.

Costa led him out the kitchen door, then around the back of the building.

"This is where the incident happened with Patrick. When he saw the dog, and the animal leaped toward him."

"And that was worth interrupting me?"

"You tell me." Costa squatted down and pointed toward a spot in the dirt. "This is where the dog—or the wolf—leaped."

"Okay. I see that."

"You only see a few dog tracks before that."

Raymond waited, wondering where the man was going with this. It better be good if it merited interrupting the work he was trying to do.

"But look here," Costa continued. "Remember we found a pile of clothing lying on the ground? Well, back here are some bare footprints leading from the house. From a large man, I'd say. Then you see the dog tracks. Right here."

As Raymond looked at the two places Costa indicated, he felt a shiver go up his spine. "What does it mean?" he whispered.

"Damned if I know."

"Give me your best guess," Raymond demanded. He didn't like where his mind was going, and he wondered if the security man's thoughts were running along the same lines.

"That a man came out of the building, turned into a dog or a wolf, attacked Patrick, then ran for the fence."

Raymond answered with a bark of a laugh. "That's impossible."

Costa shrugged. "I agree, but I can't come up with anything better."

"Let's focus on reality, not fantasy,' Raymond answered. "I want everyone alert for trouble."

"You think someone intends to snatch the girl?"

"I don't see how they'd even know she was here. Just be on the alert for anything out of the ordinary—and inform me immediately. And keep searching. I want more information," he ordered.

"Inside the grounds—and out?"

"Yes, both."

Raymond turned and headed back toward the kitchen door, walking confidently, but he couldn't help wondering exactly what had happened here last night. And he couldn't suppress a kernel of fear. He'd thought he had everything under control. But now ...

As he stepped inside, he was thinking that Costa's suggestion fit the tracks on the ground, but it couldn't be what had happened, could it?

He shuddered. He should gather the group again and go back to the interrogation, but he found it impossible to focus on that now. The mystery of the man and the big dog was too unsettling.

When he passed the group therapy room, he saw that Tory and June were still there.

June looked spacey. Tory looked furtive.

"Are we going back to the session?" June asked in a slurred voice.

"Not now," he snapped, then made an effort to appear in total control of the situation.

June still looked like her head wasn't quite screwed on straight. Tory was trying to hide a surge of relief. He focused on her, knowing that he should get on with the process of breaking her down—because once again he was thinking that he might not have as much time as he'd assumed.

Still, he was pretty sure anything he tried now would be useless, since he needed her drugged for the process to be effective.

And, to be honest, he couldn't force himself to continue with business as usual. Instead he headed back to his office, closed the door, and brought up a Google search page. Almost as if his hands had their own idea of what he should look for, he typed in "werewolf."

CHAPTER FOURTEEN

As part of his general interest in delusional behavior, Raymond had read about werewolf myths. Now he went back to some standard sources. Many of the ancient stories came from Greece and Romania, but there were examples in many different cultures. In the story about Little Red Riding Hood, some scholars suggested that the wolf could have been a werewolf, not just a wolf dressed in grandma's clothing.

He kept reading from ancient and more modern sources. The idea that the full moon exerted an influence on shape-shifters seemed to be a fairly recent invention.

He found lots of advice for spotting a werewolf in human form. Men with red hair might be candidates, also those with an index finger and middle finger the same length. And you could change a werewolf back into a man by throwing a piece of iron at his head.

Helpful, he thought, with a snort.

Everything he read was put in terms of myths or modern horror fiction. There was no suggestion that these creatures were real. But what if they actually did lurk around the world of men?

He let himself consider that possibility. If there were real werewolves, what would one be doing at this isolated facility at the edge of a national park? And why would it even want to come in here?

There was a logical answer to the first question. The Refuge was in the deep woods, a natural place for a werewolf to be prowling around. The werewolf might have been curious about the building and come to have a look. And dug his way under the fence?

But why would he be interested in Tory Robinson? Or did he even know about Tory?

Raymond had no answer, and he was still too unsettled to get back to work. Urgency still pushed at him, but perhaps it was more productive to focus on security.

The phone rang, and he glanced at the caller I.D. Gary Freemont.

Shit.

Freemont was the last person he wanted to hear from at the moment, but he could hardly refuse to take a call from the man who was funding his current project.

He picked up the receiver and said, "Raymond here."

"Are you making progress?" the brusque voice on the other end of the line said.

"She just got here."

"How long is this going to take?"

Raymond debated how to answer. He didn't want to admit they'd had some kind of intruder last night—man or wolf. And he certainly didn't want to say that Tory had figured out how to keep from taking her morning dose of drugs.

He settled for, "We're still adjusting her medication."

"Give her more."

"That could fry her brain."

"I don't give a flying fuck about her brain. I'm paying you good money to get the information I want."

"I appreciate that, but we need her coherent enough to talk."

"Yes, okay."

Should he ask why Freemont thought Tory had known Denato longer than a couple of weeks? Maybe he shouldn't challenge the man on that. Or had Tory been lying about her association with Denato?

The caller hung up abruptly, and Raymond breathed out a sigh of relief. At least he hadn't had to tell any more lies. But he knew the man was antsy, and he knew he needed results. He couldn't fake them the way he'd sometimes done at the institutions where he worked. Freemont wanted specific information, and Raymond had said he could provide it.

A shudder went through him. And what would happen to him if he couldn't deliver? He'd been so sure of himself when he'd suggested this project. Now he was wondering if he'd better be prepared to disappear.

Fuck! This was all Tory Robinson's fault. He'd thought an airhead dancer would be easy prey. Too bad she had grit and cunning. And too bad he was going to have to destroy her.

Before he could launch himself into action mode, a knock at the door startled him.

"Come in?"

It was Costa again. "Do I have authorization to bring in more surveillance equipment?"

"Of course," Raymond answered. "I was intending to tell you to do it."

"We need to go over the options and the costs."

"Aren't there standard options?"

"Yes, but there are still choices."

Raymond sighed, anxious to stop wasting time and get back to his prime target. But he forced himself to sound interested as he said, "Okay. Tell me what you want to get."

Tory glanced toward the door. She and June were still sitting in the chairs they'd occupied during the therapy session, but everyone else had left. The other patients had seemed grateful for the break. The only one out of sorts was Dr. Son of a Bitch, probably because he knew he was losing valuable time.

June was leaning back, her head tilted to the side. Tory glanced at the door, then leaned toward the other woman.

"What does Dr. Raymond want to find out from me?"

June gave her a conspiratorial look. "That's a secret."

"But you must know."

"I'm not supposed to tell you anything." She grinned at Tory. "Was Denato good in bed?"

"I have to idea."

"Of course you do. You were sleeping with him."

"No."

The other woman giggled. "Suit yourself."

Tory pressed fingers to her forehead, fighting frustration. Maybe if June wouldn't reveal the primary mission, she could still spill some information.

"Are you really a patient here?" she asked the other woman, waiting with her breath frozen in her lungs for an answer.

"No," June said, sounding a little confused.

"What are you doing here, then?"

"I work here."

Triumph coursed through Tory. That was the answer she'd expected, but she hadn't thought she was going to hear it.

"Where did Dr... . Raymond find you?"

June's eyes blinked open and stared around the room. "You're not supposed to be asking me questions."

"But we're friends."

"Friends," the other woman repeated, sounding like she wasn't sure.

"Where did Raymond find you?" Tory pressed.

"Talent agency."

Tory was about to ask another question when June sat up straighter, her eyes widening. "Do you see that?" she asked in a quavery voice.

"See what?"

June pointed toward the window. "Big animals out there. I hope they can't come in."

Tory followed her gaze but saw nothing.

"What animals?"

"A dinosaur, I think."

Oh man, Tory thought.

"And there's a flock of ... eagles."

"They can't get in." Tory switched back to business. "How long have you been here?"

"A week."

"And how long have I been here?"

June tipped her head to the side. "A couple of days, I think."

"What would you tell me if you could?" Tory tried.

"You're in danger," the woman answered, then blinked as though she couldn't believe what she'd said.

"It's okay," Tory soothed. "You said we were friends."

"How could we be friends?" June said in a vague voice. "I barely know you,"

Tory repressed a smile as she listened to more confirmation of what she'd suspected. She was trying to think of something else to ask when the light from the hall dimmed. Looking up, she saw Ted, the balding man in his sixties who was supposed to be one of the patients. He gave her a sharp look.

"What are you doing?"

She turned one hand, palm up. "Taking care of June."

"She can take care of herself."

"She doesn't feel well. Do you?" she asked the woman next to her.

"I don't feel well," June repeated vaguely.

"I'll take care of her," Ted said. "You go on. Get out of here."

"And go where?"

"It's time for lunch."

"Oh, uh, right." Tory stood and walked back to the dining room, where one of the staff was putting plates of food on the table.

"That's yours," he said to Tory, pointing to a bowl of soup.

She stared at the chunky meat and vegetables in a thick broth. No way was she eating that.

Robin and Arthur, the younger man, were already there. June plopped down in a seat and stared at the bowl of soup in front of her. It looked like Tory's, but it would be easy to put in some drug after the soup was in the bowl.

There was a basket of rolls on the table. Tory grabbed two of them.

"Hey, what are you doing?" Robin complained.

"I don't eat soup," Tory said.

"What do you mean, you don't eat soup?" Ted asked.

"Too watery."

"That's ridiculous," Robin answered.

Tory made her voice sound like that of a stubborn child. "Maybe to you."

"Put a roll back," Ted ordered.

"No." Defiantly, she licked both the rolls in her hand.

Robin stared at her. "Ewww."

Tory dipped her knife into the butter, cut off a large chunk, and slathered it on the rolls, which she then began to eat.

As everyone except June began to spoon up their soup, Tory munched on the buttered rolls.

Ted gave her a dirty look as he took one from the basket. When nobody else touched them, Tory took another.

Nobody spoke again. June was too out of it, and the others probably didn't know what to say.

Tory pushed back her chair. "Now what?"

"The dayroom," Ted said.

"Which is where?"

"Across the hall," he answered, not bothering to ask why she didn't remember.

They all went into a large room with sofas, a television set and several board games.

"Want to play checkers?" she asked Arthur.

He shrugged. "Why not."

He grabbed the checkerboard and a box of red and black disks, and they sat down at a card table.

June lolled against the sofa cushions. Robin and Ted both inspected the paperbacks on the bookshelves, made selections, and settled into comfortable chairs.

She sat across from Arthur, moving checkers around, but her mind was spinning. Dr. Raymond thought she had some information about Denato—something she really didn't know. It sounded like he thought she could identify the murderers. But the shooting had happened only a couple of days ago. And this place must have already been set up for her. The murder couldn't be it. Or what if two of Denato's men were planning to attack him—and she knew who they were? That might make sense. But she still didn't have the answer. She didn't know Denato's men, and she hadn't seen the murder.

A sharp voice from the doorway made her head jerk up.

"I understand you didn't eat your lunch, Tory."

It was Dr. Son of a Bitch, and his expression told her that the vacation from interrogation was over.

CHAPTER FIFTEEN

Tory tried not to cringe as she saw that Raymond's gaze had never left her.

"I wasn't hungry," she murmured.

"We pride ourselves on offering our patients a balanced diet here," he said. "Come to my office."

Would it do her any good to resist? What if she tried to dodge past him? But that would only make him angry. When she recalled a couple of movies she'd seen where they tied mental patients down and gave them cold-water baths—or electroshock therapy, she shuddered.

"What?" Raymond demanded.

"Nothing," she said in a small voice. She knew all eyes were on her as she walked reluctantly toward the door. June seemed to have recovered somewhat. How many hours ago had Tory switched drinks with her? Three? That might be a clue to how long the damn medication lasted.

She followed the doctor into his office, wishing she could slug him with the paperweight on his desk. But she'd have to worry about the consequences.

He gestured for her to sit in the chair she'd occupied the day before.

A knock at the door made her glance up.

"Come in," the doctor called.

One of the attendants entered, carrying a tray with what looked like the same soup they'd had at lunch. Stupid move, she thought as he pulled over a small table and set down the tray. He gave her a triumphant look before leaving.

"Eat," Raymond ordered.

"Why don't you just inject the stuff into me?" she asked.

"What?"

"I know you're trying to drug me."

"That's a paranoid thought," the doctor shot back.

"But true."

"Eat."

She dipped her spoon in the soup and took a small swallow. It was rich and meaty, but she thought she could detect a taste that shouldn't be there. Shuddering, she put down the spoon. "I'm not hungry."

"But you will eat your lunch."

She spooned up a little more, sipping tentatively, thinking about June seeing dinosaurs in the yard. The doctor's eyes stayed on her, and she was forced to take a little more and then a little more. How long could she string this out before he came over and held her nose to force her to drink?

Another knock at the door gave her a small reprieve. It was one of the security men. "I've got the specs you wanted," he said to the doctor.

"Not now. Just do it."

"I want authorization for the expenses."

"All right," Raymond muttered, standing up and starting toward the desk.

As the doctor passed her, Tory stuck out her foot, connecting with his lower leg. He stumbled, catching himself on the little table in front of her. As he righted himself and let go of the table, Tory gave it a push, and it went over, spilling the soup on his beautiful Oriental rug.

He spun toward her, his eyes blazing. "What the hell do you think you're doing?"

"I didn't do anything."

"You stuck out your foot. Then you knocked the table over."

"You knocked it over."

"That's a paranoid thought," she said in a mild voice.

She saw him struggling to banish his angry expression. Turning from her, he marched to the desk, where he signed the paper the man had brought. As he handed the paper back, he said, "Send someone in here to clean the rug."

"Yes, sir."

The doctor remained standing with his back to Tory while she sat in the chair with her heart pounding, wondering what he was going to do. Finally, he turned and faced her.

"I think the best thing is for you to go back to your room for now."

She fought not to let her relief show.

"But you did give me an idea," he said. "A shot of medication will be an excellent idea."

The words felt like a sudden torrent of ice water had splashed down on her. Lord, no!

Raymond turned again, picked up the phone and spoke in a voice too low for her to hear.

In a few minutes, three of the attendants came into the room. One had a bucket and several terry cloth towels. The other two walked toward her, lifted her up and set her on her feet. Then they marched her to the door, into the hall and toward the stairs.

Moments later, she found herself in her room, starting to feel shaky and disoriented. She had eaten a little of the soup, and she recognized the symptoms. The drug was working on her.

She turned to face the door, waiting for Raymond, but he didn't come in immediately.

The cell phone on one of the men buzzed, and he stepped into the hall to answer it. Then he gestured toward his companion, and they both stepped out of the room.

Tory was left alone, but for how long?

* * *

Raymond had intended to prepare a shot for Tory, although he did have the problem of how much to give her. She'd eaten a small amount of the soup, and it could be dangerous to mix medications. He didn't really care what that would do to her in the long run, but it might not be productive right now. If he put her out, he wasn't going to get any information at all. Probably he should wait a couple of hours.

She could stew up there in her room, waiting for him to come back with the needle.

Before he had made up his mind, there was another knock at the door.

"Come in," he called in exasperation, thinking that his office was getting more traffic than a highway rest stop.

It was Harrison, Costa's second in command.

"What is it now?"

"Where the ground is soft, we can follow the wolf tracks into the forest."

"You know where the animal went?"

"It may take some time to find out. But Smith is an excellent tracker. He can probably follow the trail—if we don't get that rain."

Raymond thought about the pros and cons. Sending one of the men would leave them short-staffed, but if they could find where the animal had gone, that might solve a major problem.

"Okay, send him," he said, thinking that success would depend on several factors.

How far had the animal traveled? And what if he'd walked through a stream or something to disguise his route? Would an animal be smart enough to do that? Not if it really were just a dumb beast, but a werewolf would have human intelligence.

Raymond wanted to laugh at that last thought. How could you believe in werewolves in the modern world? Or any world. They were just creatures of the night, conjured up in the minds of superstitious men—to explain things they couldn't account for in any other way.

Logic told him that had to be true. Yet he was left with a nagging doubt that gnawed at the edges of his conviction like the sharp teeth of a wolf.

CHAPTER SIXTEEN

Tory lay back on the bed. She should stay prepared for Raymond to come back with a hypodermic, but she simply couldn't hold her focus.

June had seen animals outside the window that couldn't be there. Tory wasn't seeing anything she thought was imaginary. The room was the same. But her vision was blurry, and she felt her senses swimming. She tried to steady herself, but she couldn't do more than grip the sides of the bed, which was rocking like a boat.

She pushed herself up, knowing that she couldn't just stay here, defenseless—waiting for the doctor to do something worse to her mind.

Staggering to the bathroom, she took the plastic cup from the sink and set it on the tile floor, smashing her foot down and shattering the plastic. It wasn't as good as glass would have been for cutting someone, but she knew it could do damage.

She took the biggest piece, careful not to cut herself as she staggered back to the bedroom and flopped down. The weapon made her feel better. If Dr. Son of a Bitch came in with a needle, she'd cut his eyes out.

But to be ready when he arrived, she had to stay awake.

She lay on the bed feeling it rock under her, clutching the glass in her hand like a talisman, praying that she could stay conscious and praying that Brand was on his way back. She'd tried to eat as little as possible of the damn soup, but the drug had apparently screwed her up anyway.

Her eyes drifted closed, and she was lost to the world.

Brand had taken down his tent and packed up his camping equipment, then carried everything back to the car. He drove out of the national forest, looking for a town large enough for a home improvement center or a hardware store. He found one in Trumansburg, and bought the supplies he'd decided he'd need. Then he drove to an outfitter where he could get some quick snacks like jerky and trail mix that they might need. A wolf could always hunt, but only when he was alone.

He tried to stay focused on business, but Tory kept invading his thoughts. What was happening at the facility? Was she safe? Would she be in the same room when he arrived?

There was no way to answer any of those questions. All he could do was try to plan for all contingencies. Which was impossible, of course.

But he kept considering problems. Like—how much would Dr. Son of a Bitch beef up security after the incident last night? And what conclusions had the doctor drawn from the invasion?

After his shopping trip, he started looking for the right spot to leave the car—a parking lot as close as possible to the fake sanatorium. In addition, he also needed a place where he could conveniently change to wolf form. After he got Tory out of that hellhole, he'd drive her to Maryland, and they'd try to figure out who had hired Raymond to interrogate her.

Once he'd parked, he wanted to get on with the rescue mission. But it was still full daylight, and he needed darkness to make his approach to the sanatorium.

He kept busy arranging supplies in the wolf backpack that he and his cousins had devised.

Finally, he was out of things to do. Knowing he was going to need his wits about him tonight, he cranked the seat back and closed his eyes. But he was too keyed up for sleep.

Just after the sun set, he locked up the car and walked into a dense patch of underbrush, where he hung the backpack on a low branch of a seedling tree before taking off his clothes and saying the familiar chant.

Coming down on all fours, he felt the freedom of the wolf form—until he had to struggle into the straps of the pack. It fell off the branch once, and he had to pick it up in his mouth and hang it up again. The second time he was more careful, and finally he was able to wiggle into it before he started out toward Dr. Raymond's madhouse.

Even though he'd driven closer, he was an hour away, and it was full dark by the time he arrived at the instillation.

His first nasty surprise was the amount of illumination. Last time it had been dark until the guards had seen the wolf. Now it was all lit up, like a baseball stadium for a night game. They were waiting for him, which made him wonder what other plans they had made.

He circled around the fence, studying the compound, and located the generator that was supplying the place with electricity. He could take it out, but not yet.

As he moved along the perimeter, he looked toward the caged balcony where he'd first seen Tory. He'd hoped she'd be waiting for him, but he saw no one up there. Was she being cautious, or had something bad happened?

His chest contracted painfully. He couldn't find that out until he got inside.

He drifted back into the woods and found a thicket where he was screened from the compound. Reversing the process he'd used earlier, he used branches to help ease off his backpack. As he started to say the chant of transformation in his mind, he saw a man moving through the trees, gun in hand, and he understood with a flash of dark insight that he'd underestimated the response to last night's incident.

Was this the only guard in the woods, or were there more? Whatever the answer, he'd better take care of this guy before he did anything else.

He moved silently through the underbrush, his wolf senses on alert as he circled around in back of the quarry. He was just about in range when he stepped on a small fallen branch that snapped under his weight.

The man whirled, and Brand chose to spring, taking the man down before he could fire. Tonight there was no reason to hold back. This bastard had signed on to help keep a helpless woman captive while a sadistic doctor tortured her.

Brand went for the throat, chomping through flesh and bone, allowing himself to unleash his savage anger.

When the man went still, Brand grabbed the back of his shirt, dragging him into the thicket where he had intended to change form. The guy would be missed. But how long before he was supposed to report in?

The only thing Brand could do was move up his timetable. He snatched up the backpack he'd left on the ground, then trotted farther from the compound where he found another suitable tangle of underbrush.

After making sure no one was watching, he went through the ritual, standing as he gained his human form. Quickly he opened the backpack and took out a shirt, pants, and shoes which looked a lot like what the guards were wearing.

He pulled them on before heading for the fence, watching for guards as he planned his next moves.

Timing was everything now, and he was glad he'd been careful to pack the knapsack in the order he thought he'd need equipment.

He pulled out a cigarette lighter, then the fireworks he'd bought in town. After lighting the fuses, he walked rapidly around the property, dropping rockets at various locations.

Small explosions tore through the night, and he saw men exiting the gate and running toward what they assumed was an invasion force. As they vanished, he used the wire cutters to make a hole big enough to slip through. His next stop was the generator, where he disabled the "on" switch.

The interior and exterior lights in the compound instantly went off, and he heard shouts from inside the house.

"What the hell just happened?"

"Turn on the lights," a sharp voice ordered.

"They're not working. It must be the generator."

"Then fix the fucking thing."

Out here, there was no ambient light, except from the stars and the half moon.

But Brand's night vision was well above average. As his eyes adjusted to the darkness, he saw men stumbling around and flashlight beams cutting through the darkness. How long would it be before someone discovered that the outer defenses had been breached?

In the confusion, he slipped to the underside of Tory's balcony. He'd be horribly exposed, but going through the house would be too dangerous now. Instead he used the hook and rope he'd brought to quickly pull himself up to the balcony level. Hoping the guards were still focused toward the woods, he cut a hole in the wire that caged her. This mesh was thinner than the main chain-link fence, and he was able to make a fairly large cut, then pull the edges apart. After he'd slipped through, he pulled them back into place so that a casual inspection wouldn't reveal his presence. Taking the wolf's pack with him, he crossed the balcony and eased the sliding glass door open. In the shadows he could see Tory lying in the bed, and the terrible knot in his chest eased. They hadn't moved her, thank God.

Now he had to get her out of here—and fast because the whole place was on alert.

"Tory?" he called.

There was no answer.

CHAPTER SEVENTEEN

Brand moved cautiously toward the bed. The first time he'd come here, she had attacked him. This time, he hoped she was expecting him, but he had no idea what chemicals they'd pumped into her mind.

As he called her name again, her eyes blinked open and focused on him, but he couldn't tell if she knew who he was.

"Tory," he whispered. "I came back, and now we have to get out of here."

She pushed herself up, and he saw something in her hand reflect in the moonlight. As she stared at him, she raised her arm, and he could see that she was holding a sharp piece of plastic.

His breath stilled as he watched her, wondering what she was going to do.

She blinked and turned her hand, staring at the plastic, then at him.

"Brand?"

"Yes."

"I prayed you'd come back," she murmured.

"I said I would."

She stared at the makeshift weapon again and let it drop to the floor. "I was going to cut anyone who came into the room."

"Good for you."

He leaned down and reached for her, folding her close. She stood and clung to him, and the sensation of holding her in his arms again was almost too much to cope with. He wanted her, more than he had ever wanted another woman in his life, yet he knew that the two of them were in terrible danger—and he must stay focused if he was going to get them out of this death trap.

When he eased away, she made a sound of protest.

"We have to go. Now."

Before he could say more, he heard the sound of the door lock turning. There was no time to make any plans. He sprang forward, flattening himself against the wall in back of the door. Tory stayed rooted to the spot where she'd been standing.

Two men came into the room. One was a security guy. The other was the man he'd seen at her door last night. When Tory saw him, she drew in a quick breath.

"Dr. Raymond?" she asked in a quavering voice, and Brand wondered if she was terrified or acting the part.

Both men were facing her, unaware that anyone was standing behind the door.

"What are you doing up?" Raymond asked.

Brand could see her trying to collect her wits. "I ... heard something."

"Nothing to worry about. We're going to move you to a secure location."

"No," she said, her voice sounding vague, but he was sure now that she was faking it.

"Let's go," Raymond.

"You don't know what you're dealing with," Tory answered.

"What?"

Brand could have shot both of them—and drawn half the security force running to Tory's room. Making a split-second decision, he leaped from his position behind the door, slamming the guard into the doctor.

They both went down in a heap, and Brand followed, picking up the piece of plastic that Tory had dropped and slashing it across the guard's throat. The man made a gurgling sound, his mouth opening and closing.

Raymond and Tory both gasped.

Out of necessity, Brand had kept his plans flexible. Now he had a better idea of how he and Tory were going to get off the grounds. Leaving the dying guard on the floor, he pulled the doctor up and spun him around as he jabbed a gun into the small of his back. "If you call out a warning or make any false moves, you're a dead man," he said.

Raymond could barely hold his voice steady. "Please, what do you want?"

Tory had taken a step back from the man who was holding her captive here.

But as she considered the situation, she darted forward and slapped the doctor across the face.

"You bastard," she spat out. "You tried to make me think I was crazy, but you're the crazy one. Or maybe the right word is demented."

"Don't damage him," Brand said, "he's our ticket out of here."

Tory looked like she wanted to pound on the guy, but she answered with a nod and stepped back.

"She's a dangerous mental patient. You see what she just did," the doctor said.

"Don't listen to him," Tory pleaded.

"I'm not." Brand answered. "Make sure he's not carrying a weapon."

Tory began to pat him down the way she must have seen it done by cops on television. Brand could feel the doctor tensing, but he wasn't going to try anything with a gun in his back.

"Check the ankles. And up the inside of his thighs."

As Tory did, the man muttered under his breath.

When Tory stepped back, Brand began to speak again. "This is what's going to happen. We are going downstairs. I'm going to play the part of the guard, and you are going to order your men to open the gate. Then we're driving out of here."

"No."

"Fine." Brand clicked a bullet into the chamber. "Then you can die right here."

"No. Wait."

"We're not waiting. We're leaving. You will walk in front of me. Tory beside me. One false move or word from you, and I'll drop you," he said, hoping the tone of his voice made it clear he was telling the absolute truth.

Brand spared a glance at Tory to make sure she was wearing shoes. Then they all started for the door.

No one was on the upper floor. "Hold up," Brand ordered as he surveyed what he could see of the ground floor.

"When we get down there," you tell your men that you've personally decided to move Ms. Robinson to another facility because this one has been compromised. Do you understand?"

"Yes," the doctor bit out.

They started down the steps with Brand still jamming the gun into the doctor's back and Tory sticking next to him.

A man came running down the hall, weapon drawn, but he stopped short when he saw the trio.

"Tell him what to do," Brand ordered in a voice he knew wouldn't carry beyond the doctor's ears.

"Open the front gate," Dr. Raymond said.

"Sir?"

"I said open the front gate." He hesitated for a moment before adding. "This facility has been compromised. I'm personally taking Ms. Robinson to a safer location."

"Yes, sir." The man ran off to obey.

"Do you have the car keys?" Brand asked.

"No."

"Where are they?"

"I don't know."

With his free hand, Brand gave the doctor's ear a savage twist.

He cried out.

"The keys," Brand prompted.

"In the car."

"They better be."

The three of them walked out the front door and toward a Lincoln Town Car. Ahead of them Brand could see the gate opening.

"You will drive," Brand said. "I will be in the front seat beside you where I will have a clear shot if you try anything funny. Do you understand?"

"Yes."

Brand could see guards gathered around, watching the three of them move toward the car. They were almost home free when the spell broke.

"That's not Patrick," one of them called out. "What happened to Patrick?"

As the guards began moving toward them, Brand swung Raymond around. "You're right. I'm not Patrick. But I have a gun in the doctor's back. If you get any closer, I'll shoot him."

The men kept their distance.

"Tory, you're going to have to drive," Brand said. "Check for the keys."

She made a strangled sound but opened the door of the car and slid behind the wheel.

"The keys?"

"Yes."

He waited while she started the engine. Keeping hold of the doctor, he pushed him into the backseat and followed.

"Go," he said to Tory. When he glanced toward the gate, he was thankful that nobody had closed it.

She put the car into gear and headed through the fence. But they had barely gotten out of the compound when the guards began shooting, not to kill anyone in the car but to stop the vehicle, Brand assumed.

He heard bullets hitting the trunk, then the tires.

"Shit."

"Out," he shouted to Tory. "Head into the woods."

He debated what to do with Raymond, then shoved the man out again, holding him as a shield.

The shooting stopped, and Brand walked backwards toward the woods, still holding the doctor.

"If you come after us, he's a dead man," he called, glancing behind himself to make sure he was following Tory.

As he walked, he was pulling a roll of duct tape from his knapsack. When they had disappeared into a darkened thicket, he paused to hand Tory the gun.

"Cover us,"

The blood had drained from her face, but she did what he asked without question, holding the weapon as he taped the doctor's hands behind him, then tore the man's shirt, ripping off a piece to use as a gag, which he stuffed in his mouth and secured with more tape.

He pulled their captive along, but it was clear that the doctor was slowing them down, probably deliberately, hoping that his men would catch up and kill the guy who had managed to get Tory out of the madhouse.

Brand stopped and secured Raymond to a tree, then bashed him on the side of the head. The wound began to bleed almost immediately.

Turning, he saw the look of horror on Tory's face.

"Head wounds bleed a lot. It's worse than it looks."

"Are you going to kill him?"

"No. Eventually, they'll come after us. And when they find him, that will slow them down again." He turned and stepped away from the doctor, lowering his voice. "Plus, if he's dead, I can't find out what the hell he wants with you."

110

When she started to speak, he shook his head. "Later."

He adjusted the small pack onto his shoulder and led Tory farther into the woods, heading for his car. It was a mile away, and if they could get to it, he could drive them out of here. Now he was reconsidering his overall plan. He'd tried to rescue Tory on his own. As he walked, he fumbled in the pack for the phone, thinking that this might be the right time to call Decorah Security and tell them he needed some assistance.

But when he tried to make the call, he found there was no cell tower reception in the immediate area. Or maybe the guys back at the compound were somehow jamming it.

Tory gave him a worried look. "What?"

"I can't call for backup. We'd better hustle." He gave her a concerned look. "Are you all right."

"I guess I have to be."

Still, when she stumbled on a root, he grabbed her arm in time to keep her from falling.

"Sorry," she whispered.

"You're doing fine," he answered, hoping it was true.

"Where are we going?"

"My car. It's not far."

Well, not far for him. It might seem like miles away to a half-drugged woman.

"How do you feel?"

"Glad to get out of there."

"Yeah."

He led her through the woods, being careful not to leave an obvious trail. Several times they had to detour around bramble patches. He wanted to ask Tory what they had done to her during the day, but he couldn't quiz her now because he had to save all her energy for walking.

Every few minutes, he glanced back, glad that he saw none of the guards was following yet. Still, he was sure they would be coming soon, and he and Tory had better keep up a good pace.

The wind had picked up, and he knew that they were pushing against a rainstorm. A few drops had begun to fall as they reached the parking lot where he'd left his car.

He breathed out a sigh when he saw the vehicle through the trees, the top reflecting moonlight. But as drew nearer, the relief turned to anger. Someone had slashed his tires and scraped the paint on the sides with a rock. He stopped short, searching the woods for movement.

"Christ."

"What?"

"Somebody's vandalized the car. Wait here."

He left her in the shadows under some trees as he surveyed the area, wishing he could change form and use his wolf senses to make sure the area was clear.

He saw no one, probably because they hadn't stuck around to watch the camper or hiker return to his disabled vehicle. He wanted to loose a string of curses, but there was no point in wasting the energy.

Instead, he made contingency plans. He opened the trunk, taking out some of the supplies he'd brought for his camping trip but knowing that he shouldn't try to carry too much.

He wished he had a rain jacket for Tory, but he hadn't brought one because it wasn't something a wolf would need.

When he beckoned to her, she came forward, her horrified gaze on the car as she took in the situation.

"Who would do that?"

"Jerks who think it's fun to ruin someone's vacation. Come on."

"Where?"

"Where we can get cell phone reception, and I can call my friends."

"They live around here?"

"Unfortunately, no. But they can get here pretty fast," he answered, trying to mentally estimate the time it would take to launch a rescue operation from Beltsville, Maryland.

With no better alternative, he led Tory in the general direction of the main road out of the park.

The moon was lower in the sky, and there was less light. He could see better than most people, but he could tell Tory was having trouble watching her steps.

As he led her away from the car, he kept to the woods.

When they'd covered about a quarter mile, he stopped and tried the phone again. This time he got reception.

"Decorah Security," a voice answered, and he knew it was one of the new agents who had drawn night duty.

"This is Brand Marshall."

"I thought you were on vacation."

"I was. Something came up. I got into an unexpected situation."

"How can we help?"

"I'd like to be picked up. On the double. I've got a kidnap victim with me, and we're being pursued by armed men. If you can send a helo, that would be perfect."

"To what location?"

"I'm in the Finger Lakes National Forest, and I'm on the move. You'll have to key in on my cell phone."

"Okay."

"I can't give you a landing site yet."

There were no more questions. Decorah Security would be here as soon as they could. Until then, he and Tory would have to dodge Raymond and the security men.

CHAPTER EIGHTEEN

As soon as Brand put away the phone, the fat drops of rain that had been plopping lazily down turned into a torrent, hitting the forest with force.

He pulled Tory close, trying to shelter her with his body, but that was impossible.

He could take the cold rain, but after a few minutes, he heard her teeth chattering. The forest had been dark. Now the clouds overhead and the curtain of water coming down made it hard to see ahead of them, and he picked his way carefully through the woods, thinking that no one from Decorah would be able to land in this torrent.

"How can you see anything?" Tory murmured.

"I have good night vision."

"Maybe it will help us."

"Maybe," he answered, wondering if the security men back there had night vision goggles.

It would be nice to think the rain would halt the search, but he knew Tory was too valuable to simply give up in the face of a little bad weather. They'd do what it took to find her, even if it meant sloshing through driving rain.

That knowledge kept him moving. He glanced at Tory. Her blond hair was plastered to her head and shoulders. Her shirt was almost transparent with water, and she moved along like a robot, putting one foot doggedly in front of the other.

Through the rain and trees, he saw a building. It looked like a small cabin.

"Can we stop there?" Tory asked.

He was sorely tempted—not for himself, but for her. Had he put enough distance between themselves and the pursuers?

He simply couldn't take a chance.

"We'd better not," he answered.

She looked disappointed but also resigned as she plodded on beside him, and he knew she had given over control to him. He'd gotten her out of the clutches of Dr. Son of a Bitch, but she still wasn't safe.

Silently he cursed the rain that was slowing them down. Desperate to make as good time as possible, he was focusing on the forest ahead when disaster struck. One minute Tory was walking beside him. In the next, she was careening forward, screaming as she went down.

He made a frantic grab for her, but she'd stumbled onto a long incline. As she went tumbling down a steep slope covered with wet leaves, he charged after her, barely staying on his feet as he struggled to catch up.

Ahead of him, he could see her snatching at trees, trying to stop her death slide. But the bark was too wet for her to catch on.

He put on a burst of speed and caught up, grabbing her arm, stopping her downward plunge just in time. Ahead was a sheer drop-off at one of the ravines in the area, and he heard rocks falling, hitting ground far below.

She looked at him wide-eyed, then looked over the edge into the rocky gorge below. "My God," she gasped. "You saved me. Thank you."

"Are you okay?"

"I don't know."

When he helped her up, she winced.

"What happened?"

"I think I twisted my ankle." She pressed down gingerly.

"Can you walk?"

"I think so." She gave him a sick look. "Do you think anybody heard me scream?"

"I hope not," he answered, thinking that they had better put some distance between themselves and this particular hill.

He held her upright, then found a broken branch which she could lean on.

They began to make their slow way up the hill. He kept scanning the crest, looking for trouble. They had gotten about halfway up when he froze. Above them on the ridge he could see a man with a rifle standing at the spot where Tory had tripped and started her near fatal slide down the hill. She'd left a trail of scattered leaves, a route that was easy to follow.

Brand pulled her down.

"What?"

"Someone's up there. With a gun," he answered, looking back again.

The man had vanished. Probably he was going to alert the others, which gave them a little time. But not much.

He led Tory to the right, both of them keeping low and putting about fifty yards between themselves and the trail she had gouged in the leaves and mud.

He parked her behind a tree and belly crawled to the edge of the cliff, looking out into space and feeling a stab of anguish when he thought of what might have happened.

She was safe for the moment, but unable to walk fast now. Could he find a safe place for her?

About fifteen feet below the drop-off, he could see a shelf of rock.

As quickly as he could, he came back for Tory. "There's a ledge down there where I can hide you."

She looked doubtful but followed, dragging in a sharp breath when she saw the narrow shelf of rock below them.

"You think there's room for us down there?"

"I think there's an overhang," he said, hoping it was true and not a trick of the shadows.

He opened his pack and took out a length of rope, which he looped around an outcropping of rock that hung off the edge. After testing his weight, he lowered himself down the rock face, easing onto the ledge where he saw what he'd been hoping for—a depression like a shallow cave. Not only would it hide Tory, it would shelter her from the rain, which was still coming down.

"There's a place for you down here," he whispered. "Grab the rope and come over."

Her face contorted. "You think I can?"

"Yes. You're a dancer. Your arms and legs are strong."

"I'm afraid of heights," she whispered.

"Don't look down."

He knew she didn't want to do it, but without wasting more time, she reached for the rope. He waited with his heart pounding until he could grasp her hips and help her the rest of the way down, guiding her into the overhang.

She breathed out a sigh of relief when her feet touched solid rock. He did, too.

"Good job," he murmured.

"Thank God I'm not dizzy anymore."

"You were?"

"Yeah."

He clasped her to him, and they clung together.

"You'll be okay here."

"We're going to hide from the guards?"

"I'm going to leave you here while I take care of them."

Her eyes widened. "There are a lot of them. How are you going to do it?"

"I won't do anything stupid," he answered as he turned away to rummage in the pack and pulled out a dry shirt. "Put this on." Next he took out one of the power bars he'd bought. "And eat this. It will help your strength."

She looked like she wanted to protest.

"Don't argue. Leaving you where it's safe is the only thing to do." As he spoke, he handed her his phone. "If Decorah Security calls, tell them I've left you to go after the bad guys following us." He paused for a moment. "And if I don't come back, call them."

"Brand!"

"I'll be okay."

"You just said you might not come back."

"I will," he said, punching out the words. "That was—just a precaution." He swallowed hard before adding, "I'll leave the rope in place so you can get back up by yourself."

"Don't leave."

The fear in her voice tore at him, but he gave the only answer he could. "I have to."

She reached for him again, wrapping her arms around him. He should ease away before it was too late to get behind the bastards up there. Instead he pulled her into a fierce embrace, his hold on her tightening. He closed his eyes, memorizing the feel of her body against his, sliding his hands up and down her back, then clasping her bottom, torturing himself with the need for her.

"You never told me your last name."

He laughed. "Right. It's Marshall. Brand Marshall."

She murmured the name, and he was sure she thought she'd convinced him to stay here with her. But that was impossible with the goon squad closing in on them.

Still when she raised her face, he lowered his, their mouths coming together for a frantic kiss. He understood she was desperately trying to keep him with her, but he knew he had to leave while he could still climb over the edge of the cliff unobserved.

He'd found a good hiding place for Tory, but he had to eliminate the threat to her.

When he pulled away, he saw the panic in her eyes.

"Back in a flash," he said, hoping it was true as he shouldered his pack.

"Get under the overhang and stay there," he told her as he reached for the rope.

When she'd moved back into the shadows, he started up, stopping before he reached the top to look around. When he saw a man silhouetted against the sky, he eased below the edge again, waiting with his heart pounding for the guy to come charging down the hill. After long seconds, he looked again, and the figure was gone, but Brand knew he had very little time to get out of there without leading the trackers directly to Tory.

He pulled himself up and flopped to the ground where he kicked leaves around the base of the rope, then slithered along the edge of the bluff, putting distance between himself and Troy before starting up the hill, staying low.

Raymond's men had made surprisingly good time, which meant they must have an excellent tracker with them. Too bad about that. And too bad they hadn't been drugged and tied up any time recently. He knew that had slowed Tory down.

Staying low to the ground, Brand climbed partway up the incline, keeping his eye on the top of the ridge. Although none of the searchers was in view, he couldn't count on staying hidden for long.

He found a tree large enough to hide behind and laid down his pack, then started stripping off his clothing. When the wet fabric clung to his skin, making it difficult to get the shirt off, he cursed and resisted the impulse to rip the damn thing off. He was going to need it later.

When he had finally stripped to his bare skin, he looked around, hating his current vulnerability. And it was only going to get worse in the next few minutes.

But he had no choice besides changing to a wolf. As a man, he didn't have a chance against a large party of

119

hostiles. As a wolf, his odds were a lot better. Too bad he didn't know exactly how many guards Raymond had brought along.

Grim-faced, he began to say the chant of transformation. He pushed through it, hurrying the change, feeling pain shoot through his muscles and tendons as he forced the change with a speed he had never thought possible.

It was still raining as he dropped to all fours and sniffed the air before emerging from behind the tree. He could smell the bastards who had invaded this pristine wilderness. If he had to guess, he'd say there were five or six of them. Long odds, but if Raymond was one of them, he wasn't going to be much help to the rest.

Brand circled to his right, making it easily to the top of the hill, and spotted a huddle of men. They looked wet and uncomfortable.

What were they waiting for? Probably Raymond, he decided when he didn't spot the doctor. The captain of the team would want to be in on the capture—even if he'd already proved he wasn't an asset in a tactical situation.

Brand moved cautiously closer, slipping from tree to tree, watching the group. The rain was letting up, which increased his visibility. But it gave the trackers the same advantage.

Still, they were only humans, looking for a man and a woman on the run. The woman was hidden and Brand was a creature of the forest now, well equipped to deliver some nasty surprises to the men who were hell-bcnt on hauling Tory back into captivity. And one of the wolf's chief advantages was silence. He didn't have to use a gun to take these bastards down. He could pick them off one by one, and the rest of the group wouldn't even know what was happening.

Raymond had let Smith lead the search party, and at first he'd struggled to keep up with the others. Finally he'd acknowledged that he was slowing the team down and ordered the main group to go on ahead. They could tell him if they found anything.

When the walkie-talkie in his hand crackled, he pressed the receive button, hoping for good news.

"What?"

"I think I found something," Costa answered.

"You have them?"

"We think we know where they are."

"Send someone back for me." As he spoke, he felt like someone had just given him a shot of amphetamine.

This was a lot better than when Smith had come back empty-handed in the afternoon—saying that the wolf must have taken a route through a stream. But it seemed that the man's tracking skills were paying off tonight. Smith was like a bloodhound or an Indian guide from the Wild West, and he'd followed a trail that no one else would have even seen. It had led to a parking lot, occupied by a car with the tires slashed.

Raymond had sucked in a breath when he saw it.

"What happened?" he asked Norland, the man who was keeping pace with him.

"It looks like vandals."

"You don't think it's a trap?"

"No. I think we caught a break," Norland answered. "It looks like the guy was set to drive her out of here, but not now."

Raymond had paused to make a note of the license plate. He'd get a contact he had in the police department to check it out. Then he'd have a better idea why a guy he'd never seen before had fought his way into a very delicate situation. He'd been thinking about werewolves of all things. But this was a man with a car. Was he a friend of Tory's—and she'd somehow sent a message?

That was impossible—not when the only landline was in his office, and cell phone use was restricted. Which left the possibility—that the man had stumbled into a situation he didn't like and had decided to rescue a woman in trouble.

The guy had somehow managed to get inside the compound and wrest Tory away. But now they were closing in, and he was out of luck.

That left out the part about the wolf. Raymond shook his head, unable to fit the animal into the picture.

When Harrison came running through the woods, Raymond pushed back his wet hair and tried not to look like he was winded from all the walking.

"How far behind are we?" he asked.

"About a quarter mile."

He gritted his teeth as he and Norland hurried to join the others.

His security men looked up as he approached, guns drawn. When they saw the familiar trio, they lowered their weapons. They were standing in a circle near the top of the hill. He didn't have to actually be here. After they'd freed him from his bonds, he'd been tempted to go back to the Refuge and medicate himself with a stiff drink.

But he'd pushed that thought out of his mind immediately. Slogging through the wet woods had no appeal, but it was the only way to be in on Tory's capture. Besides, nobody was going to humiliate him in front of his employees like this and get away with it.

As he joined the circle of men, he could tell by their faces that they were excited.

Smith gave him a direct look. "I heard a scream a few minutes ago. Then I spotted a new trail broken through wet leaves down a steep slope. Up until now they've been careful. This is different."

"A trail?" he asked, his voice sharp. "What if it's a trap?"

"That's possible, but it's more like someone tripped and took a slide down that hill. They could be injured."

"And the bastard who kidnapped Tory could be down there with a gun, waiting for us to follow."

Costa, his chief of security, agreed. "We should spread out and approach with caution. You stay up here."

"What if it really is a trick?" Chambers asked.

"Like how?" Raymond snapped.

"What if they slid a log down the hill to make it look like they tripped and fell?"

Raymond considered that, then turned to Smith. "Show me what you found."

The tracker led him about fifty yards farther on and pointed to a streak on the ground running toward the edge of a ravine. The displaced leaves and long sweep of mud certainly looked like someone had taken a quick slide down the hill.

After several moments, he said, "Okay, send a couple of guys down. But be careful."

CHAPTER NINETEEN

Brand got as close as he could to the guards and Dr. Raymond, who had come huffing up to join the main party, looking like he wished he had a golf cart to take him through the woods.

One of the men was pointing down the hill where Tory had taken her slide. Others were following the direction of his outstretched arm. Obviously they were going with the most likely explanation, that she'd taken an unexpected ride down the hill—and maybe gone over the edge.

Brand thanked God that he'd left Tory fifty yards farther along the edge of the cliff.

The wolf counted the men in the party. He could see five, but there might be more. Could he take them all out? If that was the only way to save Tory, he would have to do it.

He'd brought men down as part of a rescue operation like the one at the Hamilton Labs a few months ago, but he'd never killed one while in wolf form. He knew his cousin Ross had done it once, and sworn never again—then been forced to take out the man who had kidnapped his mate.

Brand was in a similar position now, only it wasn't just the guy he'd killed back at the Refuge. It was seven, and the only way to save Tory and himself was to eliminate them one by one—silently before they realized what was happening. Luckily a wolf didn't need a gun. He only needed his teeth and claws, backed up by skill and cunning.

Two of the security guards went down the hill, following Tory's rough slide, and Brand prayed that they wouldn't figure out that she was fifty yards to the east. The other stalkers fanned out, guns drawn, searching the woods in case she had avoided sailing over the cliff and come back up.

Carefully planning his strategy, the wolf selected the man to his far right. Staying parallel with his quarry, he slipped from tree to tree as the man looked for signs of the fugitives.

Silently moving closer, Brand kept pace with him, lurking in the shadows, waiting for the right moment. It came when the man stepped into a depression in the ground and was thrown slightly off balance. With his target at a disadvantage, the wolf sprang, knocking the guy into a bed of leaves, teeth slicing into the skin at the back of his neck. He made a low sound and tried to get the gun into firing position. Brand clamped down on his wrist, and he dropped the weapon. Brand flipped him over, and he sprawled on the ground, his eyes full of shock and fear as he stared up at the animal that had taken him down. Brand chomped again, severing bone and blood vessels. He kicked the gun away and waited until he was sure the man wasn't getting up again. He didn't allow himself to dwell on what he had done. He simply went off in search of his next target.

The guards had spread out to cover as much ground as possible. The next man Brand encountered was also by himself, edging cautiously down the hill, careful of his footing in the wet leaves. Again the wolf used the natural surroundings to good advantage. When the man was close to a rock outcropping, the wolf leaped on his back, slamming him into the jagged stone barrier and at the same time sinking sharp teeth into his gun arm, biting and shaking the limb until it went limp.

125

The man tried to fight for his life, but his struggles were of no use against a wolf determined to save the life of his mate. Brand finished him off and faded into the woods, considering his next move.

Tory was still shivering in her wet clothes, and coping with the aftereffects of the drugged soup the doctor had forced her to drink. She'd thought she was finally back to normal mentally. Then she'd realized she was acting dumb as a box of rocks.

Like now. Brand had given her a dry shirt from his pack and she was still wearing her wet one. She glanced up, making a wry sound. None of the guards was up there watching her, and if they were, she'd be in worse trouble than having them see her half naked.

Brand was another matter. She wanted him to see her that way. And not just half naked. A picture flashed into her mind—the two of them as God had made them, rocking in each other's arms. It warmed her, and she let herself enjoy the sensation for a moment—until reality intruded.

A twig snapped. Then she heard the sound of stealthy footsteps approaching along the top of the cliff.

It could be an animal, but she didn't think so. It sounded like a person treading cautiously. And it couldn't be Brand. If he was coming back, he'd let her know it was him. Which meant it must be one of the guards trying to sneak quietly through the leaves as he searched for her.

While she listened to the man getting closer, she fought panic, struggling to keep her thoughts coherent. Brand had left the rope up there tied to a boulder because she might need to come up by herself. But was it hidden well enough so that it wouldn't give her location away?

If the guy saw it, he could come down here and capture her—or tell the others where she was. Unless she acted first.

In her fogged mind, she knew that either option was a risk—but she decided she wasn't going to huddle on this ledge praying for invisibility. Standing, she was relieved to find that her twisted ankle felt almost normal. Next she grasped the rope and tested her hold. When she felt secure, she used her hands and legs to pull herself up, taking Brand's advice not to look down. Nearing the top, she moved cautiously, inching up until she could barely look over the edge. One of the goons—the guy who had taken her to breakfast this morning—was about twenty yards away, moving slowly along the cliff edge. She could tell by his deliberate pace that he hadn't spotted her. She ducked down, grasping the rope tightly with her legs and hands, thankful that she had the muscles to hold herself in position.

Her heart pounded as she braced her feet against the rock wall below the cliff edge and waited for the guy to come closer. As he moved slowly and deliberately forward, she wanted to scream at him to hurry up before the muscles in her arms and legs gave out.

After an eternity, he was finally almost even with her.

She heard him pause, then mutter aloud, "What the hell is a rope doing out here?"

As he shuffled closer to the cliffs edge, bending to look down at the man-made intrusion into the landscape, she shot up one arm, grabbed his ankle and yanked with all her might.

She had the advantage of surprise. When he made a startled sound and tried to jerk out of her grasp, she held on with all her strength, shaking his leg and pulling him off balance.

Cursing, he wheeled his arms, desperately trying to keep himself from plummeting into the ravine, but there was nothing he could grab.

He toppled off the edge, his scream echoing through the forest as he fell toward the bottom of the chasm, then landed like a sack of oranges on the rocks below.

Tory was frozen in place for several moments. Rousing herself, she slid back down the rope, her hands burning as they scraped along the rough fibers. She was shaking now, totally shocked by the reality of what she had done. She had planned her moves and pulled a man off into space. Probably he was dead. Or if not, he was horribly battered. But he was one of the guards who had done Dr. Son of a Bitch's bidding, like driving a woman crazy was just a normal job. He'd known what he was doing, and finally it had come down to one choice—his life or hers.

The others must have heard the scream, but they didn't know his location. She prayed that they would think he had slipped and gone over the edge of his own accord.

Looking up, she saw the length of the rope dangling along the side of the cliff. Quickly she pulled as much of it as possible under the rock ledge, then huddled under the overhang, listening intently for signs that more guards were coming. When her teeth started to chatter, she remembered she was still wearing the wet shirt. Pulling it off, she quickly slipped into the dry one that Brand had given her.

As soon as it touched her skin, Brand's unique woodsy scent filled her nose, then drifted to the back of her throat and from there into her brain. Her eyes fluttered shut to better appreciate the sensation. It felt almost like he was holding her in his arms, protecting her. But she couldn't keep up the illusion. He wasn't holding her. He was out there—in danger because of her. At least she'd evened the odds a little by eliminating one of the bad guys.

Brand heard a long, desperate scream ringing out in the night.

Oh Lord, was it Tory?

He told himself that was impossible. It must be one of the guards—going over the edge. As he ducked behind a rock outcropping he heard two men moving toward the drop-off. His wolf's ears pricked as he listened to their frantic talk.

"Chambers must have taken a nosedive over the cliff edge."

"Where was he exactly?"

"Don't know."

"Chambers," someone called.

There was no answer.

After several more shouts with no reply, one of the men said, "He must have gone over."

"Slipped the same way the woman did."

"She's probably at the bottom of the cliff, too."

"Any chance he's still alive? Somebody should have a look."

The men stayed huddled together. Neither made a move toward the ravine. Probably they were afraid to risk it now that one of their number had gone over. And it bolstered the theory that Tory had also taken a header into space before they'd arrived on the scene.

Another voice rang out from above.

"I heard a scream. What happened?" It was Raymond who was apparently not willing to chance his footing on the slope.

"Chambers went over."

"How?"

"We figure it was an accident." One of the men started up the hill toward the doctor. "Probably that's what happened to the woman. They both slipped on the wet leaves.

"Don't make that assumption," Raymond snapped, his tone giving away his exasperation. "Keep looking."

The order was followed by a couple of weary sighs from the men.

"What about the guy who was with her?" one of them asked.

"You'd know it if he was still around. He's long gone," the doctor answered, probably assuming Brand would cut his losses and run.

One of the guards looked around the area. "What about Smith and Gerard? Where are they at?"

Probably the two men Brand had killed. He saw the remaining searchers exchanging uneasy glances as they thought about why two of their companions hadn't come running at the sound of the scream.

"They must be too far away to hear what's going on," the doctor answered, giving his men more wishful thinking instead of leadership.

"I don't know," one of the remaining guards muttered. "What if something's happened to them?"

"Like what?"

"Like the guy got them."

"How could he?" Raymond asked. We haven't heard any shots fired.

Neither man answered, but Brand would bet the two remaining men wanted to cut their losses and get out of the woods. Too bad for them that they couldn't simply refuse to continue the fatal exercise.

Raymond spoke in a low voice, issuing orders, and the men separated again, resuming the search pattern.

Brand kept to his original plan, which had worked pretty well the first two times. Silently he stalked the man who was farthest to the right, waiting until he was out of sight before springing from behind a tree, going for the killing bite again. This time the man's gun discharged. The shot missed Brand, but it brought the other guy running. Brand left the man on the ground and weaved into the trees, heading uphill.

He heard Raymond call out as footsteps pounded toward the fallen guard.

"What happened?"

Seconds later, the man answered, "It's Gerard. His neck is ... all cut up,"

"By a knife?"

"By an animal."

"Jesus."

"Suppose that's what happened to Smith? Remember we saw a wolf at the compound. Maybe the guy is working with it."

The doctor didn't contradict the speculation, but apparently he wasn't willing to give up yet. "Give it another half hour."

"Okay," the guard with the doctor answered, but when Brand followed him, he saw that the guy was leaving the area—heading back the way the search party had come.

Raymond tried to hurry up the hill, slipping on leaves as he went, wishing there were some hiding place that he knew was safe. Things weren't going the way he'd planned. He felt vulnerable in the middle of the woods. In the rain. He knew he should have stayed back at the Refuge—for safety's sake. But if he hadn't accompanied the search party, he knew the men would have given up by now and come back with their tails between their legs. Or maybe they wouldn't have come back. Maybe they would have been afraid to admit their failure and would have put distance between themselves and the facility.

He cursed under his breath, wishing that was an option for him. What the hell was he going to do if the men didn't find the girl? How could he report to Freemont that a stranger had come into the compound and spirited her away?

As he tried to imagine the mobster's reaction, he shuddered. He'd accepted a job from a very dangerous man. At the time he'd been buoyed by past successes and sure he could deliver the information he'd promised. Now he was considering his exit strategy in earnest.

He didn't even know how many of his men were left. What if he called off the hunt, went back to the Refuge, and took the money he'd already been paid.

Then what? He'd be on the run for the rest of his life unless he could find some wealthy patron who could protect him.

And what about his standing? If word got out about this failure, his reputation was in the toilet. But did that matter if he could save his own life—then start again? Maybe under another name. It would take time, but he'd done it once and he could do it again.

Yes, perhaps that was the best approach. Freemont had no way of knowing about the girl's escape yet—unless someone back at the sanatorium was a spy.

He shuddered. He'd thought of that before and dismissed the notion. Now he knew it could be a crucial obstacle.

Brand worked his way around in back of the doctor. He could see the man moving away from the cliff edge, probably wishing he'd come in a car so that he could jump inside and lock the doors. The guy was a coward. And a bully. He apparently enjoyed inflicting mental pain, as long as he knew nobody was going to interfere with his plans—or turn the tables on him.

Brand stalked him as he moved away from the scene of the carnage. Earlier he had flirted with the idea of sparing the man's life so that he could get some answers from him. But Brand had been fighting the stalkers on his own for what seemed like hours, and his energy reserves were dwindling. Better to finish this quickly so that he could get back to Tory

"Kimmel, you're with me," the doctor called out,

Nobody answered, and Brand figured he was talking to the guard who had taken off a few minutes ago.

The doctor finally stopped shouting, pulled a walkie-talkie out of his pocket and spoke into the instrument.

"Smith, report."

There was no answer until the doctor got to Patrick.

"Sir?"

"Where are you?"

"A half mile away, I think."

"Get back here."

"Yes sir."

The doctor found a large tree and pressed his back against the bark, probably to keep himself upright. It was tempting for Brand to prolong his fear, but the guy named Patrick was heading back.

Brand circled around in front of the doctor. As the man sensed movement in front of him, he lifted his head, spotted a large gray form facing him, and gasped in shock and dismay.

Their eyes met, and the doctor's expression made Brand think of a character in a horror movie who realizes he's going to be the next victim. Still, he had enough guts to speak—although he couldn't quite hold his voice steady.

"Who are you? What are you?"

Brand bared his teeth in a low snarl.

"You understand me?"

Brand nodded his head.

"Are you ..." The doctor paused as though the very question was too much to cope with. Finally he finished, "Are you the man who ... took Tory away."

Again Brand nodded.

The doctor caught his breath. Then he finally remembered that he had a gun in his hand and raised his arm, but he looked like the weapon was as comfortable in his grip as if he'd been holding a wiggling snake.

Brand moved in a flash of motion, dodging to the side, then charged forward, taking his quarry down from the left, then going for a killing wound to the throat. The man tried to call out. Brand sank his teeth in, just as a bullet struck a few feet away.

It must be Patrick. Shit, the guy had come back on the double. But the guard couldn't take a close shot without risking hitting his boss. Instead he was trying to scare the beast away.

Good luck with that.

For the second time during the eternity while Tory had been waiting on the ledge, the sound of a gunshot shattered the night.

She jumped up, every muscle in her body tense.

She wanted to scream Brand's name. She wanted to climb up the cliff again and find out what had just happened. But she knew she couldn't make herself a problem for him. She had to stay where she was.

Almost unable to cope with the agony of waiting, she paced back and forth on the ledge, her hands balled into fists as she struggled to keep herself from going insane.

Dr. Son of a Bitch had tried to do that. His methods were a lot less successful than this torture.

A sound startled her, and she realized it was the chirp of the phone Brand had left with her. It wasn't loud, but it could give her away.

Quickly she pressed the receive button.

"Brand?" a voice asked.

"No. This is Tory," she answered, keeping her voice low.

The tone of the person on the other end of the line turned sharp. "Where is Brand?"

"He's going after the men who were following us."

"And where are you?"

"He left me on a ledge down the side of a cliff."

"How long has he been gone?"

"I don't know," she answered in frustration. "Maybe for hours. Or maybe not that long. I can't tell."

"Okay. Give him a message. We're on our way, but the rain has delayed us. It could be several hours before we reach your location."

"Yes, all right."

"Have him call in as soon as he can."

"Yes."

The connection snapped off, and she stared at the phone, thinking that the man on the other end of the line might not have trusted the information she was giving him.

Brand grabbed the man's collar and dragged him into the woods, using him as cover while he fled. He dropped the limp body as he reached heavy underbrush and faded into the trees. Several bullets followed him, but it was clear that the man had no idea of his target and was simply shooting blind.

The guard gave up, and Brand heard a walkie-talkie crackle.

"This is Patrick. We have a situation here. The wolf got Raymond. I assume the doctor's dead." The man raised his voice as he said again, "I repeat, I think the doctor's dead. "

One man answered. The one named Kimmel who had been on his way out of there.

"That's it? Nobody else?" Patrick asked.

None of the rest made their presence known.

"Key in on my location," Patrick said, backing up against a tree near where the doctor had stood and moving his gun from side to side in a two-handed grip.

Brand watched as Kimmel came plodding out of the forest.

"It's just you and me?" Making no mention that he'd been about to clear out.

"Yeah."

"And you saw what happened to the doctor?

"Yeah, that wolf I saw the other night came back. It was chewing on Raymond when I got here, but I couldn't take a shot with the animal right on top of him. It got away." He swallowed hard. "Well, it dragged Raymond with him. Like it knew to use him for cover."

"You're shitting me."

"No." Patrick looked around. "What about the intruder and the girl?"

"Screw them. Let's get the hell back to the loony bin. The doctor's dead. He's the one who wanted the girl."

"Yeah."

"We can collect our stuff and see what else we can find. Or we can just leave."

"We gonna take the doctor's body?"

"Why should we?"

"Just asking."

"Without Smith, do we know which way to go?"

"Yeah," Kimmel answered. "Approximately."

They were still discussing the best route to take as they headed toward the parking area where Brand's car had met its unexpected fate.

As he watched them disappear, he wanted to lift his face to the night sky and howl, but he stifled the impulse because he knew Tory would ask him about the wolf.

He waited to make sure they hadn't changed their minds, then headed back to the spot where he had left his clothing. Behind the same tree, he reversed the process, transforming from wolf to man. His wet clothes lay on the leaves in a sodden heap. He grimaced as he pulled on the shirt, then he went back to one of the men he'd killed, stripped off the man's pants and put them on. They were wet, but not as wet as the ones he'd discarded.

After getting dressed, he wondered what someone was going to think when they came upon this scene of carnage, Brand shook his head. He had no tools to bury these guys. The best he could hope for was that a predator would finish what he'd started. It was a cynical thought, but he hadn't been the cause of the fight. And he hadn't killed any men for sport. Only to protect his mate.

His mate.

She was his, and he wanted to start making plans for the future. But he knew that would have to wait.

He'd like to think she was out of danger now. But he couldn't say that for certain. With the boss gone, the guards would have no reason to go after her—or to stick around the sanatorium. But someone had hired the doctor to get information out of a woman who had witnessed a murder.

Maybe Tory would have a clue about what it was. And maybe she would be as deeply in the dark as Brand was himself. But he knew she wouldn't really be safe until they figured out why she'd been brought to the Refuge—which meant starting with Raymond's records.

He stopped at a stream and washed his face, then rinsed out his mouth and spit, washing away the taste of blood. It didn't bother him, but he knew Tory would wonder why he'd gotten blood in his mouth.

He began working on the story he was going to spin her as he headed cautiously back to the drop-off.

Yeah, what exactly was he going to tell her? That he'd ripped out the throats of the guys in the search party? He was sure she was going to love that. And as he went back over the past few hours in his mind, he didn't like it much either. It had been a savage night's work. But it had been his only option if he was going to save her.

He'd been in a kill or be killed situation. And if he'd been taken out, his mate would have been in a world of trouble.

"His mate." This time, he said the words aloud, feeling a surge of wonder as he let the reality sink in.

With an almost giddy anticipation, he moved along the cliff to the ledge where he had left her.

CHAPTER TWENTY

From the ledge on the cliff's face, Tory strained her ears. She'd heard nothing for a long time. Now she detected something. It sounded like a person or an animal moving along the edge of the drop-off again.

Was it Brand? Or was it one of the security guards who had been hunting them all night. She'd taken care of one of them; now she thought she didn't have the strength to climb up the rope and do it another time.

Brand, Brand Marshall, she shouted inside her mind, praying that it was him.

She couldn't call out; all she could do was pick up a grapefruit-sized rock and clutch it in her hand, her breath shallow as she waited for disaster.

"It's me."

The voice startled her, and she realized she hadn't dared to hope that he would make it back.

"Brand. Thank God." The rock she was holding clattered to the ledge.

She saw him come down the rope, first his legs, then the rest of his body. When he landed on the stone surface, she ran to him, clasping him in her arms.

"Are you all right?" he asked.

"Yes. Are you?"

"Fine."

As he held her, his mouth lowered to cover hers for a long hot kiss.

"What happened up there?" she asked when the kiss broke.

"I picked them off one by one, until the two guards who were left figured it was better to cut their losses and run."

"What about Raymond?"

"He's dead."

She caught her breath. "I heard shots. Did you shoot him?"

"No, that was a couple of his men shooting at me."

"But you're okay?" she asked, needing reassurance as she ran her hands up and down his arms.

"Yes."

"You fought them?"

"Yes, but I had to be silent, so they wouldn't know what was happening." He hesitated for a moment, then went on. "I cut the doctor's throat—like I did some of the others."

She swallowed hard, trying to picture it. "You ... eliminated all of them with a knife?"

"Mostly. I think one slipped and went over the edge of the cliff."

"I pulled him over," she whispered and heard him catch his breath.

"You did?"

"He was coming along the edge. I was afraid he'd see the rope and call the others. He did see it, but I had already climbed up and was waiting for him. I grabbed his leg and yanked him off balance."

He stared at her.

"You think I shouldn't have killed him" she whispered.

"Of course you should. And I think that was brave as hell."

She gave a little nod.

"But you're okay?" he asked urgently.

"Physically. Mentally—not so much. I never thought I'd kill anybody."

"You did what you had to—to save yourself."

She had started to shake in reaction, and he stroked her and kissed her, murmuring reassuring words until she felt more in control.

He eased her down, and they both sat with their backs against the rock wall.

"How did you get so many of them?" she asked in a thin voice.

"They spread out to search for us. I started picking them off." He made a low sound. "I can operate pretty much like a ghost when I have to."

"Like the way you got into the compound."

Before either of them could say more, the phone gave a low chime, and Tory startled.

"Oh! I forgot. Someone from ... Decorah Security called you. They didn't like it that you weren't here. They told me to tell you to call."

When she handed him the instrument, he pressed the talk icon.

"This is Brand."

Tory couldn't hear the voice on the other end of the line.

"No, I'm fine." He glanced at her. "I'll give you the details later."

Again, the other person spoke.

"Yeah, there are bodies... That would probably be best."

Again he listened for several moments.

"I understand. We're on a ledge at a place where there's a drop-off. We'll wait here for you. When you reach the area, we can climb up."

He clicked off, and turned to her. "The rain delayed them."

"They told me."

He looked up at the overhanging rock. "This is as good a place as any to wait. It's dry and nobody's likely to stumble on us here."

140

She watched as he reached into the pack and brought out a thin blanket which he draped around her shoulders. It was surprisingly warm.

"I didn't even know that was in there."

"It will help now."

"You too." She pulled at the end so it reached around him, and they sat together.

"Thank you," she murmured, "for getting me away from Dr. Son of a Bitch."

She saw his face harden.

"Son of a Bitch is right. If I'd tried to imagine the scenario back at that funny farm, I couldn't have come up with anything like it in a thousand years. Thank God I found you at that place."

Everything had happened so fast that they'd barely had a chance to talk. Well, they could have done it on the escape route if she hadn't needed all her energy for putting one foot in front of the other. Now she bubbled with questions.

"What were you doing up here?" she asked.

"I was taking a break from work, if you can believe that."

"Why?"

"I was restless. I felt like I had to get away for a while, and I picked this area for a camping trip. My dad and I had been up here when I was a teenager, and I liked the park."

"That's right. You told the guy on the phone that we're in a park?"

"Yes, the sanatorium is on the edge of the Finger Lakes National Forest."

"Oh." She shuddered. "I don't want to think about the sanatorium. Not now."

"You'll have to ..."

"Not now," she said again, turning to him and pressing her lips to his. "I want to forget about it for a little while. Please."

"I have to keep guard," he said in a gritty voice.

"We're safe."

141

"I'll be sure of that when my friends get here."

Needing to be as close to him as she could get, she switched her position, straddling his lap, the intimacy making it very clear what she wanted.

He made a strangled sound. "Don't."

"You don't want to?" she asked, moving against the erection that had sprung up as she settled onto him.

"Of course I do. But this isn't a good idea."

"Why not?"

"For the reasons I gave you," Brand managed to say. He was dizzy with desire, and suddenly all he could think of was claiming this woman for his own. But he couldn't have what he wanted—not yet.

Still, when she leaned forward to kiss him, it was impossible not to respond. He ran his hands up and down her back, then slipped them under the back of her knit shirt. When he realized she wasn't wearing a bra, he felt jolt of need.

"Ah, God, Tory."

"I'm right here," she answered with a little gasp.

He brought his hands around, taking the weight of her breasts in his palms, entranced by the feel of her. When he skimmed his thumbs across her swollen nipples, he heard her drag in a strangled breath.

"That's so good."

It was for him too. He had never wanted a woman more and never been more aware that he couldn't have her—not until he had brought her to safety.

But he couldn't stop himself from touching her, kissing her, loving the small sounds of pleasure she made.

She was his mate, even if she didn't know it yet. He understood that without rational thought. They had spent only hours together, but he knew they would be together for the rest of their lives—unless she was too afraid to accept him.

That thought sent a wave of desperation through him. Wanting her to know how good it would be between them, he slipped his tongue into her mouth and was gratified by her heated response. The need to bind her to him almost wiped away his ability to think about anything besides mating with her. She was his, and he wanted her to know it.

At the same time, in some corner of his brain, he realized that he had to stop. This was not the time and place for the ultimate intimacy.

But was it possible to stop when the blood coursing through his veins felt like it would burn him from the inside out?

The need for her tore and clawed at him, but he had to master it. Teeth gritted, he pulled his hands away from her breasts and pressed them to the hard stone below his body. Immediately, her eyes snapped open, and she gave him an uncertain look.

"Brand?"

As she asked the question, she moved her sex against his erection, driving him to the edge of insanity. Still, when she reached for his belt buckle, he stopped her.

"Don't."

"You don't want to?"

"You know I do."

"But what?"

"We can't. Not here. Not now."

Ignoring the sharpness of his need for release, he shifted her farther down onto his legs, relieving a little of the pressure building inside his body. But it was impossible to separate himself from her completely. Could a werewolf bind his mate to himself without the two of them having intercourse?

Perhaps that was what he hoped when he reached his hand into the front of her sweatpants and panties and found the folds of her sex. She was slick and wet for him, and he burned to drag her pants off—and his.

Instead he caressed her intimately, as possessive emotions leaped inside him.

He dipped his finger inside her, then stroked up to her clit, learning what felt best to her as he gave her pleasure.

Her hips moved as she thrust herself against his hand and away, and he drank in every subtle shift of her body and every sound she made.

"Brand."

"I have you."

He felt her movements become more urgent, heard her cry out as he moved his hand faster, feeling small convulsions against his fingers, convulsions that traveled outward, making her body shudder. She went limp against him, her head dropping to his shoulder.

Knowing he had given her so much pleasure sent a wave of satisfaction through him.

Her eyes blinked open, and she raised her head, staring at him, looking confused and embarrassed.

She flushed. "I ... shouldn't have done that."

He laughed. "Did I give you a choice?"

The flush deepened. "There's always a choice."

"Right. And I wanted to do what I could with you—for now."

"But ... what about you?"

"I have to make sure we stay safe."

"And I tempted you almost beyond endurance."

"Almost."

He was glad she didn't know what it cost him to lift her off his lap. Still fighting the needs coursing through him, he pulled the blanket around her shoulders and settled her against himself again.

"I'm sorry," she whispered.

"Don't be. You've just been through a horrible ordeal, and that was the first taste of the pleasure I'm going to give you to wipe the bad stuff away."

"Oh, Brand. I'd still be back at that horrible place if you hadn't found me."

He pressed his lips against her hair, drinking in her scent as he settled her head on his shoulder. "Try to rest."

"You, too."

She closed her eyes and leaned into him, but neither one of them was really relaxed—for different reasons.

Still, he was glad he had taken a step in binding her to him.

"I want ..."

"What?" he asked.

"I said that out loud?"

"Yes."

"I want to be with you," she answered lamely.

"You are with me."

"I mean ..." Her voice trailed off.

"If you mean forever, you have me for as long as you want me," he answered, hearing the gritty tone of his own voice.

She drew in a quick breath, turning her head so she could meet his gaze. "You hardly know me. You never would have met me if ..."

He held his breath, waiting to hear the end of the sentence.

"If you hadn't stumbled on that asylum—and believed that I wasn't crazy. I mean, didn't I seem ... screwed up?"

"I heard them talking. I knew you were their captive—and that something weird was going on. But it wasn't your fault."

He stroked his hands up and down her arms, raising goose bumps on her skin.

"What kind of man would do what you did for me?" she asked in a small voice.

"Anyone with an ounce of moral fiber."

She raised her head. "I don't want to think about Dr. Son of a Bitch. Tell me stuff about yourself. Where did you grow up? Did you have a big family?"

That seemed like an easy question. At least part of it.

"I grew up on a farm in Howard County, Maryland. My family raised sheep, and my dad repaired machinery for other farmers. We did a lot of outdoor stuff."

"That's why you're so good in the woods."

"Yeah."

"It sounds like a good life."

"Some of it was very good."

She tipped her head to the side, studying him. "What was the downside?"

"My dad was strict. It was either his way or not at all."

"You had brothers and sisters?"

He swallowed. "I have a couple of brothers."

She must have seen something in his face. "You get along with them?"

"We're not close," he clipped out. He didn't say that two other Marshall boys had died when they made the change from boy to wolf—and a sister had been born dead. He didn't tell her that was what had happened with werewolf families down through the ages. To turn the conversation away from himself, he said, "What about your family?"

"I'm from Pittsburgh. My dad works for the government. My mom's a housewife. We had a pretty middle-class life. I went to a coop nursery. My mom was a Girl Scout leader. She baked cookies. She decorated my room in classic girl style."

He nodded, picturing her as a toddler, then a teenager.

"I have one younger sister, Anna," she went on. "We're still pretty close. My parents encouraged me to do what I wanted in life. Unfortunately."

"What do you mean by that?"

"Instead of going to college, I studied dance, and I was good at it. That's how I ended up at the Midnight Club." She made a snorting sound. "Or maybe getting the job had more to do with my looks than my dancing ability."

"Your looks are stunning."

She touched her hair. "I'm a mess."

146

He laughed. "You can wash your hair soon. And you know a top New York nightspot wouldn't have hired you if you weren't good."

She sighed. "I guess. But I'm not cut out to be a professional dancer. I'd decided I was going back to Pittsburgh to teach at my friend's dance studio and start college part-time. That will give me a lot more career choices. I should have left before I met Denato."

"None of what happened is your fault."

"I should have had the guts to say I wouldn't go out with him. Does it make sense that I knew my manager would have been angry if I'd said 'no'? I mean, I saw it as part of my job."

"Uh-huh."

"The only good thing about all this is that I met you."

"I wish we could have done it the easy way."

"Like how?"

"If I'd come into the Midnight Club, would you have dated me," he teased.

She tipped her head up and looked at him. "I would have been drawn to you. But maybe I would have been a little frightened, too."

"Why?"

"You're pretty intense."

He tightened his hold on her, cradling her in his arms.

He wished he could simply let her relax after her ordeal, but now that she'd brought up the subject, he knew there were questions he had to ask.

"Do you know what Dr. Son of a Bitch wanted from you?"

He felt her shudder. "He said a couple of things," she whispered. "In the therapy session, he saw we were going to explore my role in Johnny Denato's death. But there must be more to it. He had the fake patients waiting at the Refuge before I got there."

"How do you know?"

"June—one of them—told me. I switched drinks with her at the snack break, and she got loopy."

"Clever."

"I keep wondering if Raymond had something to do with Denato's death, and that's why the interrogation was all set up."

"That's a possibility."

"He said I was wanted by the police for questioning."

Brand's voice rose. "That's a damn lie. His death didn't even make the papers."

"It didn't?"

"No. Somebody must have cleaned it up."

She hitched a breath before going on. "I think his saying that was just to scare me into cooperating—so I'd spill some confidential information about Denato."

"Why?"

"Because I was going out with him."

"Would Denato confide in a woman he was casually dating?"

"He certainly didn't confide in me. He was charming but distant. I tried to tell Raymond we had a casual relationship, but I don't think he believed it—or didn't want to believe it." Her gaze turned inward as she thought about the past few days. "I told him I'd only seen the man for a few weeks. He seemed surprised about that—like he thought it was longer. Or somebody told him it was longer." She raised her face and looked into Brand's eyes. "Do you believe that?"

"Yes."

"Why?"

"Because you wouldn't lie to me."

"How do you know?"

"I think there won't be any lies between us," he answered, but he wondered what was written on his face.

"Wait. Are you lying to me about something?"

"No," he said. "But I want to figure out how to tell you some things about myself."

"Bad things?"

"Things that might frighten you."

148

"Oh," she whispered. "Is that why you're tense?"

"Yeah. But something you can count on. I would never hurt you. Never."

She searched his face for a long moment before answering, "Okay."

The way she said it made him wish they were already past the hard part. But one thing he did know. At least he could give her a better life than werewolves had been able to offer their mates in ages past. His cousin Ross's wife was a geneticist, and she'd made a big difference in the survival rate of children born to members of his clan.

Before Tory could ask him any more questions he didn't want to answer, he heard the sound of a motor in the distance, and then Brand's phone rang. He answered it immediately, relieved to get out of the conversation—at least for the moment.

"Yes?"

"This is Frank. We're going to land in a clearing about a quarter mile from your location. Can you walk there?"

He glanced at Tory. "No problem with walking a quarter of a mile?"

"I think that's okay."

He conveyed the information, then clicked off, suddenly feeling weird about introducing his boss to his lifemate— when she didn't even know about her new status. He stood with a jerky motion, feeling her eyes on him.

"Is something wrong?" she asked.

"No," he answered, pulling the rope taut. After making sure it was secure, he hauled himself up, then reached down for Tory, grasping her hand and pulling her upward.

When she'd reached the upper level, he clasped her to him, stroking her back before turning her loose.

"Okay?"

"Yes."

"Then let's get out of here."

As they started off, he kept his arm around her.

149

When she asked, "What's wrong?" he knew she could feel the tension gathering inside him.

"I've been thinking about what we have to do next, and it's something you aren't going to like."

CHAPTER TWENTY-ONE

Tory's head whipped toward Brand, and the look on her face made his chest tighten painfully.

"I thought I could trust you," she whispered. Afraid she might be going to run from him, he got ready to follow.

"You can."

Still looking uncertain, she asked, "Then what are you planning?"

"We have to go back to the sanatorium—while we still have access."

Her reaction was exactly what he had expected. "No!"

"I wouldn't ask you to do it if I thought there was some other way to find out Raymond's motivation."

"What do you mean?" she demanded, and he was thankful that at least she was listening to him.

"Someone hired Dr. Son of a Bitch to interrogate you. And if we don't find out who it is, you're going to remain in danger. Why should they give up because Raymond's dead? Do you want to spend the rest of your life in hiding? You want to never see your parents or your sister again? And do you want to put them in danger?"

"How?"

"If someone can go after you, he can go after them."

151

She went pale, and he could see that he'd gotten through to her.

"I can't take that chance."

"Then let's try to figure out what's really going on. All right?"

"I guess I have to."

He clasped her hand, and they started off, following the sound of the rotors. Finally, Brand saw the machine through the trees and picked up his pace.

Three men stood at the edge of the clearing, their shirts flapping in the wind from the rotor. Frank was in the lead, along with Mack Bradley and Cole Marshall, Brand's cousin. Ben Walker was at the chopper's controls.

Brand could feel Tory slowing down as they approached, but he kept her moving, watching Frank watch them with a satisfied expression on his face.

"Tory Robinson, this is Frank Decorah, my boss," he said. "Frank, this is Tory."

"Nice to meet you," they both said, shouting above the sound of the helo.

Then Frank added to Brand, "I knew there was some reason you were coming up here."

"You did?"

"Yeah. Kismet."

Brand would have liked to explore the comment, but the older man motioned to Cole, who came over. He also opened a channel on his satellite phone so that Ben could hear as well.

"Tory ran into a bit of a problem in New York, and she ended up at a fake sanatorium up here," Brand said, then gave them the executive summary of what they were doing up here.

Cole winced, then turned to Tory. "Lucky you hooked up with Brand." He was also giving them a close look, and Brand knew both he and Frank were pretty sure this woman was going to be Brand's lifemate. Well, he certainly couldn't talk about that now, especially since he hadn't explained anything to Tory about werewolf bonding. He knew that she felt close to him. But how was she going to like finding out that her lover was a shape-shifter.

The uncertainty on his face must have given something away.

"What?" Cole asked.

"Personal discussions later," Brand clipped out. "Right now I think we need to go back to the facility where they were holding Tory and see if we can figure out exactly what was going on." When he explained his thinking, the others agreed.

"The sooner we get in there and out again, the better," Ben said, his voice crackling over the phone.

"Can you give us the location?" Ben asked.

Brand provided some rough directions. "I'll recognize it when we get there," he said. "Plus it's the only big structure you're going to see at the edge of the park."

"What about your car?" Frank asked.

Brand grimaced. "I'll have to take care of that later. Someone will need to come up here with four good tires."

As he escorted Tory to the helo, he gave her an apologetic look. "I've got to give Ben directions; do you mind sitting in back with Frank and Cole?"

"That's okay," she answered in a small voice. He could tell she didn't love the idea, but it was probably just one more thing she didn't like at the moment.

After they were strapped in, Ben took off, and they headed east, toward the edge of the park. He looked down, watching for vehicles on the road, but he saw none heading toward the facility or away. The surviving guards must have made a quick getaway.

When he spotted the compound, he pointed, and Ben circled, then landed just outside the gate, which stood open the way they had left it. They brought along several extra weapons as they exited the helo.

Tory's pale face and drawn features told him how much she didn't want to be here.

Still, when they'd all assembled outside the fence, he said, "You can wait out here with Ben, if you want."

"I don't want to make you one man short. And I don't want to cower out here while you go in."

"Good. Then let's do it."

He kept one hand on his gun and his other hand linked with hers as they walked through the gates. If he hadn't known better, from the look of the place, he might have thought that the building had been abandoned long ago.

"How many people were here?" Frank Decorah asked.

Brand glanced at Tory, but she only shrugged. "You have a better idea than I do."

I'd say there were eight guards and at least two other staffers in addition to the doctor."

"And four fake patients," Tory added.

"What's a fake patient?" Cole asked.

"Dr. Raymond was pretending that there were four other people here for treatment—two men and two women—in addition to me. But I'm certain all of them were actors pretending to be in treatment. We all had meals together. And we had a group therapy session. He was also trying to convince me I'd been there for weeks, when I'm sure I only arrived a few days ago." She swallowed hard. "He was also drugging me. But yesterday, I switched orange juice with one of the other women at snack time, so I didn't get that dose. When I didn't eat my soup at lunch, he brought it into the office and made me eat some—until I spilled a lot of it on his expensive carpet."

Cole winced. "Nice."

"And all to find out something about a guy named Johnny Denato," Brand said.

"The gangster?" Frank asked.

Brand nodded. He looked at Tory. "Can you tell them something about what happened before you got here?"

She filled them in on her relationship with Denato—ending with his being killed in his apartment.

"Kind of strange that it didn't make the papers," Frank said.

"Exactly what I was thinking," Brand answered.

"So it's not Denato who initiated this elaborate plan," Brand added. "It's someone else, and we need to find out who that is."

"Is the client aware that Tory escaped?" Ben asked.

"We don't know," Brand said. "I assume not because Raymond and his men came after us immediately." Turning to Tory, he asked, "Can you show us the doctor's office?"

"Yes."

She started for the door, but Brand put a hand on her arm. "Let us make sure the place is really cleared out."

"You stay with her," Cole said. "We'll search."

The other men went in, and Tory stood stiffly beside Brand as they fanned out. Cole went upstairs. Ben went to the basement, and Frank took the first floor.

Tory watched him heading for the kitchen. "What's wrong with his leg?" she asked.

"He lost part of the leg in Vietnam," Brand answered. "Most people don't notice."

"I'm a dancer. I notice how people move."

"Right."

"He manages fantastically well, and he looks a lot younger than what his age must be," she said.

"Yes, we think he's got some secret fountain of youth."

"Really?"

"I'm only half kidding."

They stopped talking as Cole came back. "The basement is empty, except for some holding cells.

Tory's breath caught. "Holding cells?"

"Nobody's in them," Cole answered.

Before he could say more, Frank returned. "No one's on the first floor. But I can see the staff cleared out in a hurry.

The cook must have been in the middle of preparing a meal. He left vegetables and meat on the counter."

Ben was just coming down the stairs. "People left their stuff up there and cleared out on the double."

"When the men on the search team who survived came back and gave them the bad news," Brand clarified.

"It looks like ten rooms up there had been occupied." Cole said. "Some were doubles."

"And there's a nicely furnished bedroom on the first floor that probably belongs to the doctor," Frank added.

Cole turned to Tory. "You were locked in the room with the cage around the balcony?"

"Yes. Brand found me up there." She swallowed. "Well, maybe a wolf found me."

Brand stiffened.

"A wolf?" Cole asked carefully, his gaze swinging from Tory to his cousin and back again.

"Yes. I saw it outside on the grounds." She turned to Brand. "Did you see it?"

The question hung in the air before he answered.

"Yes."

The two werewolves exchanged glances, and Brand kept his gaze steady and as neutral as he could manage. He knew Cole was thinking, "You haven't told her yet."

He answered with a tight nod.

"What?" Tory asked as she caught the silent exchange between the two men.

"We'll talk about it later," Brand clipped out. "Right now we have to search Raymond's stuff and get out of here. Show me the office."

She hesitated, her gaze still on him, and he knew she wanted to ask questions. Finally, she turned and walked stiffly down the hall.

"This is where I woke up," she said as they stepped into the room. It held only a comfortable seating arrangement and small desk.

Not much here," Brand muttered. Stepping into the hall, he started opening doors and found one that was more of a working office.

"In here," he called, and Tory joined him.

Ben stayed at the front door. Cole went upstairs where he could watch the road leading to the facility. Frank followed Brand as he walked to the laptop computer on the desk. When he touched a key, the screen sprang to life.

"He figured he was coming right back, and he didn't turn it off. And nobody on the staff would have dared violate his privacy," Brand remarked as he began scrolling through the doctor's directory.

He found an extensive collection of information on Tory and another with employee names and positions. He also found a lot of background on a man named Gary Freemont.

"Does that name mean anything to you?" Brand asked Tory.

"No."

"I think he's the client who wanted you brought here."

Tory stopped pacing and came to stand behind him again. Frank took several steps into the room, looking at Brand expectantly.

"Apparently Freemont had heard about Raymond's specialty through a satisfied customer."

"There's a network of these guys?" Tory asked in a disgusted voice.

"Like any criminal activity," Frank muttered.

"Freemont came to him offering a lot of money if he could get information from you," Brand added, scrolling down through the file. "He was initially delighted to hook up with Raymond. But when nothing happened right away, he started getting impatient for results," Brand said.

"Impatient! I'd only been here for two days," Tory said. "I mean, trying to convince me it was longer was part of his strategy, but he couldn't pull the same tricks on Freemont."

Brand shook his head. "I guess the guy realized he'd made a bad deal."

"Or maybe he gave Raymond bad information," Tory murmured.

"Like what?"

"Raymond thought I'd been in a long-term relationship with Denato. That wasn't true at all."

Brand switched to another file. "Raymond did a bunch of research on both Denato and Freemont. It looks like both of them are—or in the case of Denato, were—into a drugs, gambling and sexual slavery."

Tory sucked in a sharp breath. "Prostitution?"

"Immigrants brought in for the purpose—with no way to escape."

Tory gagged. "Maybe that's why Denato never made any moves on me."

"I'm guessing they had an agreement to divide up the city—but Freemont wanted more."

"So maybe he's the one who killed Denato," Tory said.

Brand nodded.

Tory clenched her fists. "And I was going out with a guy who was thoroughly despicable."

"You didn't know."

"I knew I was afraid of him."

Brand scrolled rapidly through correspondence.

"Here's some e-mails where they're discussing Denato. And from the tone and content of the exchange with the doctor, I'd say that Denato and Freemont were supposed to be business partners—but Freemont thought Denato pulled a fast one on him and stole a lot of their profits." He scrolled through another e-mail. "Jesus."

"What?" she asked, leaning over his shoulder, then caught her breath. "He thinks that because you were Denato's girlfriend, you know where the guy kept his money."

She went very still. "From the questions Raymond was asking, I thought he wanted me to identify the killers. " She clamped her hand around Brand's arm. "I have no idea who they were—and I don't know about any money. So all this was for nothing."

Brand swore again. "If you're trying to come up with scenarios that make sense—Freemont had Denato killed. He sounds nasty enough to do it."

"And nasty enough to hire Raymond to make my brains leak out through my ears—based on his false assumptions."

"Yeah."

Her gaze had turned inward. "What if Freemont thinks everyone is like him?"

"What do you mean?"

"Well, if he were dating someone with a lot of money, he'd try to figure out where the loot was stashed—so he could steal it."

Frank joined the conversation. "For a lot of people, money and sex are the two big motivators."

"Don't forget revenge," Brand said.

Tory watched the exchange, then hitched in a breath. "Now that we've figured out what Raymond wanted to find out, can we split?"

"I understand why this place makes you jumpy, but give me a few more minutes. We've got a gold mine here. I want to look at more of Raymond's files."

"Can't you take the laptop with you?" Tory asked.

Brand had been so caught up in the hunt for information that he hadn't considered that alternative. "Okay, but I need to check his files to make sure I have his password."

Before he could say more, his phone vibrated. He looked at Frank, who shrugged.

"Brand here."

"This is Cole. You're right, I have an excellent vantage point up here. I can see a long way in the distance, and I have a fix on a car heading this way. The road is easy to see as it winds through the trees. As far as I can tell, there's nowhere else to go but here. So the car must be on its way to the sanatorium."

"Who would be coming here?" Cole asked.

"My best guess? Either the cops or the guy who's been trying to contact Raymond—Freemont. How long do we have to get ready—if it's him?" Brand asked.

"It's a big car, and the curves in the road are slowing it down. I'd say we have about twenty minutes before they get here."

CHAPTER TWENTY-TWO

"I'm not betting on the cops," Brand said. "This was a completely illegal operation. Nobody here was going to call in the cavalry—before they ran away."

"I agree," Ben answered. "Plus, if they thought something bad was going on up here, they wouldn't send one car to an isolated location like this. And the vehicle's not police issue. It's a honking big Caddy."

Brand crossed to the phone and scrolled through caller I.D. He saw several recent calls from Gary Freemont, starting before Brand and Tory had busted out of the facility.

"Freemont's been calling with increasing frequency."

"Can we listen to what he said?" Tory asked.

Brand shook his head. "We'd need a password to access the messages, but I'm betting Freemont was pressing for progress reports." He checked the time stamps. "A lot of the calls came in after we forced Raymond to leave at gunpoint. Now Freemont is coming here to see why the doctor blew him off."

Tory looked on the verge of panic. Then her expression changed. "We have a helicopter," she said in a breathless voice. "We can get out of here before he arrives."

"We don't know what kind of firepower he's packing," Brand answered.

"Something that could shoot down a helicopter?" she asked.

"Probably not. But we'd be making ourselves vulnerable. And we've got an advantage if we stay here."

"Like what?"

"I want to nail the bastard who hired a quack to make you think you were crazy."

"He'll see the helicopter," Tory answered.

"Raymond could have a helo, for all this guy knows" Brand said.

"We'd better hustle," Ben said.

Brand turned to him. "Right. You close the gate, then open it like you're the guard when Freemont gets here." He ushered Tory back to the office where Raymond had set it up like a place to see patients. "You will be sitting in one of the office chairs, playing like you're drugged and out of it."

She looked like she wanted to tell him to do it himself. Then with a sigh, she sat down.

He reached for the Glock he'd stuck in his waistband and handed it to Tory. "Have you shot one of these before?"

"No."

"Well, you probably won't have to. But just in case— there's no safety on a Glock. You just put your finger inside the trigger guard and squeeze."

She looked doubtful but took the weapon and wedged it down between her thigh and the inside arm of the chair.

Brand heard Cole coming downstairs, and the four Decorah agents stepped into the hall where they could confer in private.

Frank looked at Brand. "I can play Freemont. From the correspondence, I'm assuming Freemont and Raymond never met in person. But Raymond's picture might have been available."

"Just tell him you never put your real picture online. Let him think you're paranoid."

"Now the big question," Cole said. "Do we use two wolves or one?"

Brand was torn but said, "I think I have to stay in human form. Tory will expect to see me here."

"Too bad you haven't told her yet."

Brand gave him a hard look. "And you're telling me you rushed to give Emma the news?"

"No," the other werewolf clipped out.

"Let's stay focused on the current situation," Frank reminded his shape-shifters.

Both men answered with tight nods.

They continued to speak quickly, all of them used to working together in developing and improvising tactical plans.

Brand returned to look at Tory, who was sitting in the chair with her head slipping to the side.

"Are you okay?" he asked.

"No. But I guess I have to be."

Frank cleared his throat. "I may have to fake a session with you."

Her gaze zeroed in on him. "Maybe you should tell me what I'm going to reveal to you."

"Think of a plausible hiding place and tell me that's where the money is stashed."

"Okay."

Brand wanted to go to her, but he knew they were on a deadline. "Sit tight," he said as he followed Frank out of the room.

He, Frank, and Cole went to the front hall to wait for the mobster.

When the car pulled up in front of the fake clinic, Brand held his breath as he waited to see who got out.

First came two tough-looking guys in the front. One was the driver, who walked around to the right passenger door and opened it.

A short, dark man wearing a well-cut suit who appeared to be in his late fifties or early sixties got out of the back.

Okay, Brand thought. Freemont and two bodyguards.

He studied the guards. Both were tall, well-built and probably in their thirties. Old enough to know what they were doing but young enough to have a lot of physical reserve. One was going bald and had shaved the rest of the hair on his head. The other had a thick blond mop. Both were wearing suits, undoubtedly to hide the guns they were carrying.

After taking their measure, Brand focused on Freemont. He had a full head of hair that had turned gray at the temples. The solid darkness of the rest signaled that the color had come out of a bottle. His suit was more expensive than those of his men. His face was ruddy, like he spent a lot of time at the bar and in the sun.

Was he armed, too? Or was he depending on these guys in case there was any trouble.

Frank stayed at the top of the steps.

"Freemont?"

The other man nodded.

"Glad to finally meet you in person," he said, and Brand waited to see if the man was going to say they'd had drinks in New York or something.

The mobster kept his gaze fixed on Frank. And his next comment told everyone that he and Dr. Raymond had never connected in person. "You don't look anything like your photograph."

Frank laughed. "A little strategy of mine. I never put out my real image."

Freemont nodded, still studying Frank. "I tried to call you several times, but you didn't answer. Would you mind telling me what's going on?"

"I was working with our patient, and I had left instructions not to be disturbed. The staff is very good about not interrupting when I'm working."

"Okay," the mobster said.

"We've had a real breakthrough. I'm sure you'll want to hear what she has to say. Come inside."

He turned and entered the front hall as though he owned the place. And at the moment, he did.

Freemont followed. When his driver and bodyguard moved to keep pace," Frank held up his hand. "Inside, you're going to hear proprietary information."

"My men don't care about that. They go with me."

Frank kept his gaze steady. "They may not care, but I do. I'm sorry. You are the only visitor I can allow to see the patient."

Brand watched the mobster considering the statement. Finally he gave a quick nod. "All right. But this better be good."

"You're going to love it. She's like a lamb eating out of my hand."

"I'd like to see that."

Frank held out his arm in a grand gesture. "This way. I was going to invite you up here myself. You came at an excellent time."

Freemont followed him inside and down the hall, glancing into the common room and the dining room. "Quite a place you have here."

Frank shrugged. "I like comfortable working conditions. They help me get into the right mood for breakthrough discoveries."

Brand glanced at him, thinking he might be laying it on a bit thick, but Freemont seemed to be eating it up.

As they walked, Cole detached himself from the group and walked back toward the kitchen.

The mob boss was still focused on Frank. "How much did you pay for this place?"

The Decorah director didn't miss a beat. "I got it cheap. The owner committed suicide in the parlor, and nobody wanted the property."

"Oh," Freemont answered.

"Let's recap," Frank said. "You wanted to know where Denato is keeping his money."

"Not his money. My money! He cheated me out of millions, and I know the bastard doesn't trust banks. It's got to be in his condo."

Frank led the way to the office where Tory was sitting in the chair with her head lolling to the side.

She looked up languidly when the men entered the room.

"How are feeling, Tory?" Frank asked.

"Very good," she said in a slurred voice that made Brand's stomach clench. This must be the way she'd looked and sounded when the real doctor had drugged her. Turning her head, she looked at Freemont with a puzzled expression. "Who are you?"

"He's a colleague of mine," Frank said.

"I thought he might be a new patient," Tory answered in the same spacey tone.

"We were talking about Johnny Denato," Frank said.

"Yes."

"You were his mistress, right?"

Brand saw Tory stiffen.

"It's all right to admit that," Frank said in a soothing voice. "Nobody is going to think less of you."

"It was supposed to be a secret," Tory answered.

"You and I have no secrets," Frank said. "Do we?"

"No," Tory agreed, continuing the masterful performance.

"We understand each other very well."

"Yes," Tory agreed again.

But the little play was interrupted by the sound of gunshots from outside.

CHAPTER TWENTY-THREE

Freemont's reflexes were excellent. As he heard the exchange of gunfire, he did two things almost simultaneously. He reached for Tory, snatched her up and clamped her against his chest as he pulled a gun from inside his coat, which he held against his captive's neck.

She gasped, and the sick look on her face made Brand's throat clog. The scam had been working perfectly. Then everything had gone to hell in the space of a few seconds.

"Make the wrong move, and she dies," the gangster said.

"And you won't get the information you want," Frank said, his tone icy.

Brand spared him a quick glance. If he didn't know better, he'd think that the Decorah owner was prepared to sacrifice Tory.

"What the fuck is going on?" Freemont asked.

Neither Frank nor Brand answered.

"And what do you know about it?" he asked, directing the question to Tory.

"Are you here to save me?" she asked in a thin voice.

"Save you?"

"You came to help me, right?"

Brand gave a tiny nod. Way to go, he thought. That ought to confuse the bastard.

"I said, what's going on?" Freemont said. As he spoke, he took a step backwards, pulling Tory along with him.

She looked scared but determined.

There was utter silence outside now.

"I know you two are carrying. I want you to drop your weapons. First Raymond and then you," he said to Brand before turning back to Frank. "Ease your gun out of your holster or pocket. Hold the butt between your thumb and finger, then drop the weapon."

When Frank had complied, Freemont looked at Brand. "Now you."

Brand had given his gun to Tory. "I'm not armed."

"Why not?"

"House rules," Frank said. "He was in too close proximity to the patient."

Freemont's eyes narrowed, but he apparently accepted the explanation, at least about the weapons. "What is this—some kind of scam? You told me you could get the information I wanted so you could lure me up here?"

"You came up here on your own," Frank said in a level voice.

"And now what just happened outside?"

"I have no idea. Maybe your guys started something?"

"For no reason? I rather doubt it. But we're going out and have a look." He gestured with his head. "Over there, or I shoot the girl."

Both Brand and Frank moved to the side of the room the mob boss had indicated.

Brand's gaze flicked from Tory to the chair. His gun was wedged beside the cushion. But he couldn't get to it with Freemont holding a weapon to his lifemate's neck.

He prayed she was going to be okay. Christ, what had happened outside to fuck up their well-oiled charade?

A low, ominous growling noise in back of Freemont made him stop in his tracks and half glance around to see what was back there.

Knowing it was Cole in wolf form, Brand took advantage of the distraction and leaped toward the man, knocking his gun away from Tory.

Freemont whipped the gun toward him and fired, but Brand had already come in low, then jerked the man's gun arm up. He shot himself in the chest, and the mobster went still.

Brand grabbed the gun as Cole backed away.

Frank had already grabbed Tory and pulled her behind himself.

It was over in seconds.

Cole trotted toward the back of the house and disappeared. Brand rushed to Tory and took her in his arms. "Are you okay?"

"Yes."

When footsteps pounded down the hall, Brand reached to snatch the gun he'd just put down.

But it was Ben.

"What the hell happened?" Brand spat out.

"The bodyguards were taking a look around—and stumbled over a body."

"Shit. Who the hell was it?"

"I just took a look," Ben answered. "I'd say—it's the cook."

"I guess he got in the way when Raymond's men were desperate to split."

"Freemont's guys came back at me and started shooting," Ben continued his explanation. "I ducked behind their car and returned fire. They're dead."

Brand turned to Tory, who had a puzzled look on her face. "What?"

"It sounded like an animal was in back of Freemont."

There was a long moment of silence as Brand tried to figure out what to say. He was saved by Cole who must have changed to human form and pulled on his clothing in record time. His gaze flicked to Brand and back to Tory. "Actually, it was me. I'm really good at animal sounds."

"I would have sworn it was a wolf," Tory said, glancing at Brand.

"But you couldn't see him, right?" he asked.

"No. But I saw a wolf looking at me when I was on the balcony that first night."

"I guess there are some of them around here," Brand said, feeling Cole's eyes on him. What did his cousin expect him to do, confess to being a werewolf in front of an audience?

Frank stepped out of the room to make a couple of phone calls. When he returned, he jumped back into the conversation. "We should get out of here while the getting's good."

Tory cleared her throat. "What ... uh ... about the bodies strewn around?"

"A cleanup crew is already on the way," Frank answered.

"And I'll take Raymond's computer," Brand said. "I'd like to understand this whole plot better. Too bad Freemont's thugs stumbled on that body before we finished the conversation.

Brand checked the doctor's password file and swore. "Apparently he got into the system with 'mastermanipulator.'"

"Nice," Tory murmured.

He turned off the machine and closed it up.

As they started down the hall, Tory asked, "Where are we going?"

"First to Decorah Security headquarters. Then to one of our safe houses."

She drew in a quick breath. "You think I'm still in danger."

"I'm not taking any chances with you."

Probably she'd like to ask, "And then what?"

But he thought she didn't want to have a private conversation now any more than he did.

This time, there was no need for Brand to give directions. He sat in the middle of the backseat, between Tory and Cole, while Frank took the copilot's seat; and Ben assumed the pilot's position again.

As they flew toward Maryland, Brand felt Tory's head drift to his shoulder. He looked over and saw she was sleeping, which was good. She'd been through a hell of a lot in the past few days, and he knew she needed to rest.

As they came down on the helipad next to the office, she woke again and looked around, not exactly at ease.

While he'd been sitting in the backseat of the helo with Tory, Brand had been texting Frank in the front, going over further plans. Frank had given him the use of a house in the rural part of Montgomery County.

"I need the keys to the place where we're staying," Brand said to Tory when they exited.

"You're staying with me?"

"Of course. Unless you don't want me there," he forced himself to add.

"Of course I want you there."

"Good."

Frank had also texted the office, and Teddy Granada, one of the IT guys came out with the keys to the safe house, along with a set of car keys, since his vehicle was still up at the Finger Lakes National Park.

"We'll send someone up there to put on new tires and drive it back," Frank said.

"Appreciate it."

He and Tory got into the company car and started off. He could tell she wasn't entirely comfortable. They'd met under pretty strange—and intense—circumstances. Now she could be having second thoughts about going off alone with him. Which was another good reason for staying away from the subject of werewolves.

When he sighed, she must have heard him.

"What?"

"I wish we had more information about Freemont—and Denato."

"You can get more, can't you?" she asked.

"Yeah. I think Frank already put Teddy on it. He's the guy who delivered the keys."

"The one who looks like he slept in his clothes for the past few days?"

Brand laughed. "Yeah, but he's the best IT guy in the business."

"Is Decorah Security a big company?" Tory asked.

"There are about ten agents in this building and some support staff," he answered. "You met Ben and Cole."

"He's your cousin, you said."

"Right," he answered, wondered if she was just making conversation to fill the time.

After a forty-minute ride, they reached the house, which was on a private road that wound through a forest of maples and tulip poplars. Four acres around the house were enclosed by a chain-link fence topped by razor wire.

"What do the neighbors think this place is—an outpost of NSA or the CIA?" Tory asked.

"Nobody much comes up here. You noticed that the road is private. We have cameras to warn us if anyone approaches."

She answered with a small nod, and he pulled up at the gate, which he opened with a remote control, then closed behind them before he turned into the circular drive in front of the house. It was a typical Maryland farmhouse from a hundred and fifty years ago, with a lot of interior modifications.

When they stepped inside, Tory looked around in surprise. The interior walls had been removed to create a great room with a seating area in one corner, a dining room with a table for six, and a modern kitchen. The sofas and chairs were overstuffed and comfortable. The table, chests and tables were lovingly restored antiques.

"Wow," she murmured. "This is quite some place."

"There are three bedrooms upstairs. You can have the biggest one."

"Okay."

"You'll find women's clothing in the closet. Some of it should fit you. But you'll probably want to take a shower. Then maybe a nap."

"I'll start with the shower."

He took her upstairs to the center bedroom that was furnished with a four-poster bed and matching cabinet pieces. He went down the hall to a smaller room that also had a private bathroom.

After his own shower, he stuffed his dirty clothing into the trash can and found slacks and several shirts. He started to put on a knit one, then changed his mind. The guards at the facility had worn polo shirts. He switched to Oxford cloth, then spent a little time scrolling through Raymond's files. When he got to the doctor's notes on his method, he cursed as he read the cold-blooded way the man ignored any regard for the people he was torturing. His goal was to get information, and he didn't care what he did to someone's mind, as long as he got the results he wanted.

Anger surged through Brand as he thought of Tory in the man's clutches. Thank God he hadn't had her long enough to do any major damage. At least she seemed to have come out intact.

Still, he felt a rush of anxiety. After closing the computer, he hurried down the hall to her room. When she didn't answer his knock, alarm leaped inside his chest.

He reached for the knob, turned it and stepped into the room. She'd drawn the shades, and he waited for his eyes to adjust to the low light. Tory was lying in the bed under the covers and the chenille spread, with her eyes closed. As he tiptoed closer, he heard her even breathing and knew she was sleeping. He should leave her alone, he thought. She'd been through so much in the past few days that his head spun when he thought about it.

But as he started to back away, her eyes blinked open and focused on him.

"Brand?"

"You need your sleep."

"That's not really what I need."

When she held her arms out to him, he was helpless to resist the invitation. Kicking off his shoes, he eased onto the bed beside her.

She gave him a shy smile. "What was it you said about where you wanted to make love with me for the first time?"

His throat felt so thick that he could barely speak, but he managed to say, "In a nice comfortable bed."

"And here we are."

CHAPTER TWENTY-FOUR

Tory raised up a little, and Brand saw that she was wearing a lacy gown that came up high under her breasts.

He saw her watching his reaction.

"I found it in one of the drawers."

"Good choice."

He rolled to his side and covered her mouth with his. There was no pretense that he simply wanted to comfort or reassure her. Heat jolted between them the moment his lips touched hers. And when he sucked her bottom lip into his mouth, he heard her moan of approval.

When the kiss broke, she ran her hand over his shirt. "You need to get rid of this." She laughed softly. "And your pants. That would be good, too."

He climbed off the bed long enough to unbutton the shirt and throw it on the floor, then shuck off his pants and underwear in one smooth motion and slip under the covers, gathering her into his arms.

She sighed as he pressed her body to his.

In the back of his mind he was thinking he should tell her how much this meant to him. This was the first time he was going to make love with his lifemate.

"What?" she asked.

175

"What do you mean?"

"You're worried about something. Do you think Raymond damaged me too badly for a normal relationship?"

A normal relationship? If she only knew.

"No. You're a strong woman."

"Then what?"

"I want this to be perfect for you."

"That's a pretty big demand you're putting on yourself."

He swallowed hard. "Yeah."

"Don't. And if you're wondering, I'm nervous too."

"Why, exactly?"

"This is our first time together. But it's more than that. I think the two of us have ... bonded on some level that I don't understand. And I don't want to screw that up."

"Bonded?" he asked, marveling that she was the one who had used that word. For him it was so emotionally charged that it wiped out almost everything else. He couldn't be sure what it meant to her.

"Yes. But I can't explain it."

He could, but he wasn't capable of telling her the truth about the two of them. Not yet.

Did that make him a coward? He preferred to think of it as prudent. Long ago a werewolf had probably gathered up his lifemate and swept her off to his den. But he didn't want to use caveman tactics. He wanted Tory to choose to be with him.

To that end, he brought his mouth back to hers, kissing her with passion that threatened to flair out of control.

It seemed to be the same for her as her hands moved over his back and down to his butt, pressing his erection against her middle.

The world dimmed around him. He could focus on nothing besides the woman who held him in her arms.

He slid his fingers under the thin straps of her gown, playing with the silky skin of her shoulders before easing the straps down her arms, trapping them while he lowered the bodice of her gown, uncovering her breasts.

They were small and perfect, and he leaned in, pressing his face between them before swirling his tongue around one hardened nipple, loving the way it stood up in response.

She made a moaning sound, then gasped as he took the nipple into his mouth, sucking while he gently bit the hard nub.

"Don't trap my arms," she whispered. "I want to touch you."

When he'd pulled the gown over her head and tossed it away, her hands came up to clasp his head, holding him to her, stroking her fingers through his thick hair. Neither of them spoke, but words had become unnecessary. She lowered her head, her teeth digging into his naked shoulder, not hard enough to break the skin but hard enough to jolt him. Had other men brought out a streak of wildness in her, or was it only because she was with a wild creature now—even if she didn't know it?

He lifted his head away from her, focusing on the breast that he had wet.

She slid one of her hands downward, over his ribs, then onto his stomach and downward.

He kept his gaze on her face as she wrapped her fist around his erection.

When she squeezed him, he sucked in a sharp breath.

"You feel so good," she murmured

"What you're doing feels wonderful, but I can't take much of it now."

She gave him one more small squeeze before taking her hand away. He rolled her to her back and pulled down the covers so that he could admire her body as he began to stroke his hand over her curves, playing with her breasts and the swell of her hip before sliding his fingers into the curly hair at the top of her legs.

She closed her eyes for a moment, then opened them as he slid one finger lower, into the folds of her sex, the joy of touching her there again almost taking his breath away. She had been hot and wet for him the last time. It was the same now.

Only it was going to end quite differently. He slid his finger through those swollen folds and into her while he bent to claim one of her nipples with his mouth again.

"Now. Please now," she gasped out.

His gaze burned into her as he covered her body with his. Reaching for his cock, she guided him into her.

The reality of being inside her was overwhelming. He went very still, looking down at her, feeling the impact of the moment.

She kept her gaze on him, and when he began to move, she matched his rhythm. Every instinct urged him to let himself go, but he held back, waiting for her to catch up with him. He felt her moving faster, pushing for climax. And he knew the moment she reached it as her inner muscles contracted around him.

He drove for his own satisfaction, feeling a burst of sensation that burned through every cell of his body before he gathered her to him, breathing hard.

She was his now. He knew that in every fiber of his being. And all he wanted to do was love her and keep her safe.

"I love you."

"Oh Brand, you don't know how much I wanted to hear that. I knew I loved you when you left me on that cliff edge and went off to fight an army of Raymond's men."

"Not an army."

"But it was just you against a bunch of armed guys."

"And that's in our past."

"And our future?" she asked.

Deep down, he knew they had to deal with reality—at least the normal part of reality. "You were a dancer in New York."

"And I told you I was getting ready to quit and go back to Pittsburgh."

"To teach at a dance studio and go back to college."

"I imagine there are dance studios and colleges in Maryland," she answered.

Relief flooded through him. "You don't mind making the switch?"

"I want to be with you." She swallowed hard. "But what about Denato? I was in his condo when he was murdered. Aren't I a suspect?"

"No. After you left, someone swept in and took him away and cleaned up the mess. There never was any evidence of a murder."

"Oh my God," she breathed. "And the men who killed him never saw me there."

"But we still have to find out what happened."

He gathered her to him, glad that he'd been able to reassure her that she was in the clear, as far as the law was concerned.

He felt her relief as she began to reevaluate her situation and start to think about the future.

"Where do you live, exactly?" she asked.

"Actually, not far from here. I have a house I got at a foreclosure. My cousin, Ross, helped me fix it up. It's got plenty of land around it. And it's on the edge of a big park."

"Like the Refuge," she murmured.

"Yeah, but I'm not holding anyone captive there. I'm just used to the countryside. Remember, I grew up on a farm."

"Are your parents still there?"

"After Dad died in a tractor accident, my mom moved to Florida." He laughed. "I guess she decided she deserved a relaxing retirement. My brother and I bought her a condo on the beach."

"And your brother?"

"He kept the farm. Ross financed my college education. I was shopping for a job when I met Frank."

"And you hit it off."

"Right. After that I looked for a place to live." He laughed. "But I'm no decorator. You'll probably want to get some prettier furniture."

"I want to see it."

"I'd like to stay here until Decorah and I can check out the Denato/Freemont situation. Something about it doesn't add up."

"Like how?"

"The timeline for example."

She nodded.

"We should get something to eat," he said.

"Like what?"

"This place is pretty well stocked. We can have anything from pizza to Asian vegetable dumplings."

"What do you want?"

He paused for a moment, thinking that a werewolf's diet was something else he hadn't talked about. "I eat a lot of meat," he said. "I'll bet there's steak in the freezer."

"Okay. Let's go see. Cooking is something normal I can do while we're here."

They both got dressed, and he stopped in his room to get the laptop. He watched her investigate the pantry, the refrigerator and the freezer.

"How does steak, mashed potatoes, and salad sound?" she asked.

"Good," he answered, thinking he should tell her he didn't eat much salad.

She took out a couple of strip steaks and thawed them in the microwave while he sat at the table, still looking through Raymond's computer.

When his phone buzzed, he saw that it was a text from Teddy Granada at Decorah. It said, "Someone's still holding onto Denato's apartment. The condo fee for the rest of the year was just paid."

Tory turned from washing potatoes and looked at him, probably noting his thoughtful expression. "What?"

"Nothing we have to worry about right now."

She kept her gaze fixed on him. "You look worried."

"Not exactly."

She dragged in a breath and let it out. "If this relationship is going to work, we can't keep secrets from each other. Is that something I should know?"

"It's about Denato's condo. Someone is still paying the upkeep."

"Which means what?"

"I don't know."

"But you think?" she asked, and he knew she was working hard to pull the information out of him.

"Freemont thought Denato's money is hidden there, but apparently there's someone else involved. I'd better check it out."

She put down a potato with a thump on the counter. "If you're going up there, I'm going with you."

"No!" he answered immediately.

"Why not?"

"It could be dangerous."

"Then I'm not letting you go there alone. You already put yourself in enough danger for me."

CHAPTER TWENTY-FIVE

Protective instincts raged inside Brand. No werewolf would deliberately put his mate in danger. That's why they were at this safe house now.

Yet what Tory said made sense. She'd been to the condo, and even if she didn't know what she was looking for, being there would jog her memory.

He dragged in a breath and let it out. "We'll talk to Frank about it in the morning. Right now, we should eat."

She nodded and went back to food preparation, but the relaxed mood was broken, although she tried to bring it back with questions about his life and Decorah Security.

Still, the conversation inevitably turned back to Denato.

"It might not be just about money," Tory blurted as she cut a piece of steak. "I meant there may be papers there—or some information that's worth more than money."

"I was thinking that too," Brand agreed.

After dinner, he found an e-mail from Decorah Security with the floor plan of Denato's condo.

Brand called it up on his tablet, and they both sat in front of the screen, looking at the rooms.

"Did you know how big the place was?" he asked.

Tory shook her head as she examined the schematic. In addition to the foyer and the living room, which she'd seen, there was a powder room off a hallway and a well-appointed kitchen at the front with an adjoining maid's room. Farther down the hall was a small bedroom that Denato probably used as a den or office and a large master bedroom with a huge bathroom. Off the bedroom was a good-sized terrace that overlooked the park.

"A place that big in New York City must have cost a fortune," Tory mused.

"You didn't see much of it, so your going along isn't going to help a lot."

She gave Brand a hard look. "Don't think you have a chance of leaving me here."

He sighed. "Okay."

He should be thinking about business, but as she cleaned the kitchen, simply watching the graceful way she moved turned him on.

She bent to put the last of the dishes in the dishwasher, then turned to rinse out the sink. Brand stood up and silently walked behind her, trapping her between the cabinets and his body as he reached to cup her breasts.

She caught her breath, leaning back against him as his hands moved over her.

"Let's go upstairs," he said, hearing the husky quality of his voice.

"And do what?" she asked in a teasing voice.

"Hum, well I was thinking we should continue this in front of a mirror."

"Just like this?"

"Well, I was picturing both of us naked. And we wouldn't be standing. You'd be sitting in my lap. You'd have your legs spread so I could have complete access to your body—and watch exactly what I was doing."

Her breath quickened as he described the things he wanted to do.

"Then we'd better go up, while I can still walk."

"I'll be right in back of you, making sure you don't fall down the stairs," he said.

True to his word, he stayed at her back, his hands still exploring her body as they climbed the stairs.

When they reached the mirror in the bedroom, he kept his position.

"Let me watch you undress."

"Lord, Brand. I can barely stand up."

"I'll be right here," he promised, meeting her gaze in the mirror.

He loved the game they were playing, but even as he teased her, he couldn't shake off a feeling of desperation.

If something went wrong at Denato's condo, this could be the last time he made love to her.

Only nothing was going to go wrong, he told himself as he bent to nibble along the side of her neck.

He struggled not to let his fear show as she threw her head back to give him better access. He'd claimed her for his mate, and now the idea of existing without her was unimaginable.

A car pulling up outside the safe house woke Brand, and he was immediately out of bed, naked, but with a weapon in his hand.

Tory gave him an alarmed look. "What?"

"Somebody's here. You stay in bed."

It turned out to be his car, driven by Cole, who had bought new tires and driven down from New York.

Quickly Brand pulled on a pair of jeans and went downstairs.

"Thanks, buddy," he said as he walked around the vehicle. It would need a paint touch-up, but the new tires definitely put it in driving condition.

Cole was about to say something as Tory came down the stairs. Brand suspected it was a question about whether they'd had "the talk."

He gave a quick shake of his head as she stopped to look at the two werewolves.

"You want coffee?" she asked.

"Neither one of us drinks coffee," Brand answered.

"It's a family thing," Cole added.

"Then what?"

"Herbal tea."

She raised an eyebrow but continued into the kitchen where she filled the kettle and put it on a burner.

"The tea's in the right-hand cabinet," Brand said.

He took mint, and Cole took cranberry. Neither one of them told her that a werewolf couldn't deal with caffeine, or cigarette smoke, for that matter.

"And what do you eat for breakfast?" she asked, looking from one to the other.

"There's more steak. That would be good," Brand answered.

She rolled her eyes. "You want that with toast and jelly?"

"I can fix the steak," Brand said, walking toward the freezer. "You can have eggs or oatmeal, or whatever you want."

"Sure."

"My wife's used to it," Cole said.

"You're married?" she asked looking at his left hand.

He paused for a moment. "In our line of work, a ring is in the way."

"Okay," she murmured.

Brand was thinking that it would be difficult for a werewolf to change shape wearing a metal circle on his finger.

She watched him take out a couple of strip steaks and put them in the microwave to thaw.

"All of your family has strange eating habits?" she asked.

"Just the guys," he answered, then picked up his phone. While the steaks thawed, he had a quick conversation with Frank, who had already gotten the news from Teddy and talked to Cole while he drove down.

When the steaks were thawed, Brand put them in a pan and cooked them briefly on both sides, before serving himself and Cole.

Tory had fixed herself instant oatmeal, which she topped with canned fruit. When she offered Brand and Cole some, they both declined.

As they ate, the three of them discussed plans to check out Denato's condo.

"No point in making a career of driving back and forth to New York," Cole said.

"Then what?" Tory asked.

"Frank's letting us use the helo again."

Tory's eyes widened.

"It's faster," Brand said. "And Frank's made arrangements to land on the helipad at a building near Denato's place."

"And we're leaving when?" Tory asked.

"In an hour."

She pushed back her chair. "I'd better go wash my hair."

"For Denato's empty apartment?"

"For a trip into the city," she answered, then stopped short, her gaze swinging from one man to the other. "Will you put the dishes in the dishwasher?"

"Yeah, we're civilized," Brand answered.

When she had left the room, Cole looked at his cousin. "I think you need to tell her."

"You don't have to keep bugging me about it. I know I'm overdue to fess up."

"But you're afraid she'll run?"

"Or be revolted."

"A woman isn't revolted by her lifemate."

"That's reassuring."

"At least we don't have to tell them that half their children will likely die," Cole said.

"Yeah, lucky Ross found a lifemate with the skills to solve that problem," Brand agreed.

He also left to shower and change.

By the time Tory came down, dressed in jeans, a dark tee shirt, and running shoes, they were ready to drive in Brand's car to the Decorah building in Beltsville for the trip to New York.

"Cole's going with us," Brand told her. "Also Ben and Nick Cassidy, who's up from the Florida office."

When they arrived at Decorah headquarters, she saw that the other agents were dressed in brown uniforms that had the logo of a delivery company on the pocket.

As Tory eyed the outfits, Ben said, "It's less conspicuous for you and Brand to go into Denato's apartment alone. The rest of us will be deliverymen elsewhere in the building."

While Cole changed, Ben explained the plan in more detail, and she nodded in agreement. The other agents would be in and out of the building pretending to deliver boxes to another condo from a van in the alley.

They made the short trip to the city and landed on the roof of an apartment about two blocks away. The van was waiting for the group, and they drove to the alley that ran parallel to Central Park South.

When they'd pulled up, everyone except Brand and Tory put on visor caps to go with their coveralls. They also donned various facial disguises. Ben and Cole had mustaches. Nick had sideburns and glasses.

When they were ready, Ben called the front desk to say that they had a delivery for number 4C, which was two floors below Denato's unit.

The super unlocked the backdoor and watched while they unloaded a couple of boxes. But when it appeared that the delivery was going to take some time, the man went back to the basement.

"What are the people in 4C going to do with a ton of gourmet popcorn and Belgian chocolates?" Tory asked.

Ben laughed. "Hopefully, they'll like it. Or they can give it away."

"But what happens when you knock on the door?"

"We don't knock. We just slowly pile it up in the hallway. We keep our heads down, so any surveillance cameras can't get a shot of our faces. And we'll stay in touch with you by phone. You should check in every twenty minutes," Cole said to Brand.

"Got it."

Tory had tried not to focus on their next moves, but finally she knew it was time for her and Brand to go into the scene of the crime. She'd hated the idea of sending him into danger alone. But now that she was here, the reality of being here made her feel like she was stepping into her own grave.

They rode up with the other men as far as the 4th floor, then stayed on for the trip to the sixth. Once outside the elevator, they stopped to check their communications equipment.

"Brand here," he said into the phone when he reached Cole.

"I hear you loud and clear. Try Ben and have him call you back."

Tory suffered through the delay. She wanted to get this over with, and at the same time, she was glad for every second that kept her in the hallway and out of the place where she'd hidden from murderers.

Finally they had established the link, and she led Brand down the hall to Denato's door. She was thinking it should have had yellow crime-scene tape blocking it off, until she remembered that nobody had found a body in the apartment. She was the only one who had seen it.

They both pulled on thin latex gloves, and Brand turned toward the door with the set of lock picks that he'd brought along.

Tory's stomach knotted as she watched him working. Like many New York City residences, the door had three locks. He started on the upper one and worked his way down.

Finally the door opened, and the apartment of horror yawned before them.

There were no lights on inside. And when Brand closed the door behind them, Tory felt the breath solidify in her lungs. .

When she started to gasp, Brand turned to her with concern. "Are you all right? Are you choking or something."

"Just a flashback reaction. I'll be better when I get out of here," she answered, trying not to look toward the spot on the floor where Denato's body had been lying. She couldn't stop herself from dragging in a breath and took in the strong smell of bleach.

She wanted to keep her gaze straight ahead, but finally she turned toward the place where she'd last seen the gangster lying.

The body was long gone, and the floor had been scrubbed clean. Thus the bleach smell. But she imagined bloodstains in the grout separating the marble squares.

Brand touched her arm, and she jumped.

"Sorry."

"I'm nervous," she answered, unable to speak above a whisper as she listened for any sounds in the apartment. It was still as a tomb—another death image.

Brand slung his arm around her shoulder, pulling her against his side as he rubbed her chilled flesh. "I understand. I'm not so happy myself. The sooner we can finish here, the better. So where would Denato stash money and papers?"

"I was thinking about it on the ride up from Maryland." She glanced toward the living room where she'd hidden behind the drapes while the men had been going about their nasty business. With a shudder, she turned away. So far, this place was full of unpleasant memories, but soon she'd be in territory she hadn't seen before.

She was glad she had studied the floor plan the night before and had an idea of the size.

"Maybe we should start in the den. That's a logical place," Brand said.

"Why?"

"Well, he did business there, didn't he?"

"Okay."

"And if we don't find anything, we can keep going to the bedroom."

She answered with a tight nod.

The light might be dim, but it felt like Denato could step back in here any moment and turn on the lights. Except that was impossible because he was never coming back, she assured herself. She'd seen him as dead as a lion shot by big-game hunters.

Still she half expected to open a closet and have his limp and bloodied body tumble out—a pretty fanciful notion, she silently admitted.

Brand searched the closet while she opened desk drawers. He'd given her a lesson in how to do it effectively, and she felt the bottom of each drawer before she closed it.

He emerged from the closet and checked along the baseboards, then rolled back the rug and examined the floor before dragging the carpet back into place.

This was taking too long, she thought, as the phone in Brand's pocket buzzed.

When she jumped, he put a reassuring hand on her arm.

"That's the guys," he said, clicking the talk button.

"Everything okay?" Cole asked.

"Yes. We check in again in twenty minutes."

Brand put the phone back and finished searching the office. When they found nothing useful, they started for the bedroom.

Before they reached it, lights flashed on, and an angry voice called out, "I guess you can't do anything right."

Tory instantly knew who it was.

"That's Denato," she moaned.

"It can't be."

CHAPTER TWENTY-SIX

Brand silently cursed as he realized someone was between them and the door to the condo.

"Turn around," a clipped voice ordered. "And don't try anything funny."

Cole and Tory turned, and he saw a man holding a gun, which was pointed at Tory. Although the guy looked to be in his fifties, he was in excellent shape, with a trim figure and a full head of dark hair flecked with a scattering of gray.

"Who are you?" he asked, focusing on Brand.

"Tory's friend."

"How'd you end up sticking your nose where it doesn't belong?"

"She asked for my help," Brand answered, trying to buy some time.

"Yeah, to steal my money. I see a bulge under your jacket. You're carrying. Drop your weapon. Take it out slowly, and hold it between your thumb and finger," giving the same directions Freemont had used when he'd gotten the drop on them at the Refuge.

"You don't really want me to drop it, do you?" Brand asked.

"Don't be smart with me. Put it down on the floor."

192

Brand pulled the gun out of his pocket and reached down to lay it on the floor. He also pulled his phone from his other pocket and pushed the send button. He knew Denato would be focused on the weapon. And as he put the Sig down, he scooted the phone across the polished wooden floor. When Denato spun to see what was making the noise, Brand grabbed Tory and dragged her around the corner. Denato got off a shot, but they were already into the bedroom, then into the large bathroom.

"Oh God. Oh God," she moaned as he slammed and locked the door behind them.

Thank the Lord the room was the shape he'd seen in the plans, with a section of wall sticking out to block the tub from the door. Brand pulled Tory into the tub where she'd have some protection if the guy outside started shooting again. Or maybe he realized that someone might already have heard the shot.

"Lie down."

She flattened herself in the large tub. Climbing in, he covered her body with his, praying that pushing the send button would alert the others.

"That's really Denato out there?" he asked.

"Yes."

"I guess he's not dead."

"That's what everyone was supposed to think," the man's voice called out from the other side of the door. "She was supposed to call the cops and tell them I had been murdered, but instead she ran."

"And what were the cops going to do when they didn't find a body?" Brand challenged.

"I had an arrangement with a couple of patrol officers who were standing by and were going to fix that," Denato answered. "But Ms. Robinson screwed up my plans. And then she and Gary Freemont started working together. Or maybe they were already pals."

"I wasn't working with Freemont," Tory answered. "I didn't even know him."

Denato made a scoffing sound, then said. "Don't bother with the lies. I know you and him were up at some fancy refuge upstate."

Tory made a low sound.

"If you think that's what was going on, you're dead wrong," Brand said.

"Cut the crap," the gangster replied, then addressed Tory again. "I knew you'd come back. I have this whole floor, and there's a surveillance system in here." His voice had turned smug. "All I had to do was wait for you to return for the money. And I knew I could get to you before you could find my stash. It's under the floor in the bedroom. But that won't do you any good. There's no bathroom window. I've got you trapped in there. Come out, and I'll make it a quick death."

"Screw you," Brand answered.

A hail of bullets hit the door, and Brand pressed Tory against the bottom of the tub. Slugs bounced off the porcelain, but none of them could plow through the sturdy old fixture.

"Maybe the cops will come," Tory whispered.

"I wouldn't count on it. They didn't come the first time. Probably he's got this place soundproofed, too."

The observation made her look sick.

"But I have backup coming."

"Yeah, right."

When Brand started to push himself up, Tory grabbed his arm and shook her head.

He turned back to her, knowing the other Decorah agents might not get there in time. He had to save her life—even if it meant that she ran screaming from him.

He came back down and put his mouth to her ear. "He thinks I don't have a weapon.

She turned her head and whispered back. "But you do?"

"Not in the conventional sense." He dragged in a breath and let it out. "I was going to tell you. I knew I had to tell you. But I didn't know how. You saw a wolf in the woods. That was me. You said we had the same eyes—remember?"

She stared at him, and he knew she wasn't taking it in. But who would?

Brand heard the door rattle. Quietly he stood and pulled his shirt over his head.

"I love you Tory, and this is the only way I can save you," he said. Then, in a whisper, he began to say the chant of transformation.

He felt Tory's eyes on him as he shucked off his pants, still chanting, rushing through the change so he'd be ready when the bastard came in.

He kept his gaze focused on the door, but he heard Tory moan behind him.

One more shot hit the barrier. Then the door slammed open, and Denato stepped into the room.

Brand was still making the last of the change from man to wolf, and heard the mobster make a gurgling sound as he backed away from a vision he had no way to understand.

Finally, in wolf form, Brand sprang, coming in low, under the gun, smashing the mobster backwards into the tile floor, hearing his head crack. The gun fired, but the shot went wild. Brand chomped down on the man's wrist, shaking it until the fingers went limp and the gun dropped to the tile.

But Denato wasn't giving up. He raised his other hand, aiming his fingers for the wolf's eyes.

A gunshot rang out, and Denato jumped, then tried to scramble away. As he put distance between himself and the wolf, another round split the air, and Denato went still as a red stain bloomed on his chest.

Brand pawed the man, making sure he was gone. Turning, he saw Ben standing in the doorway with a gun in his hand. The other two Decorah agents were behind him.

Brand nodded at them before walking into the hall where he silently said the chant that reversed the transformation process.

He heard someone clear his throat and saw Cole holding his clothing.

"Thanks," he said as he dressed.

"No problem," Cole answered.

"Can you give me a minute?" Brand asked.

"Yeah."

"And thanks for saving our lives," he added.

The three agents walked down the hall, and Brand stepped back into the bathroom.

Tory was sitting up, her gaze riveted on him.

Wishing he could read her expression, he said, "You told me you felt like you'd bonded with me. A werewolf bonds with his lifemate. Although I don't know what happens if she decides she can't cope with a werewolf mate."

He reached out a hand to her, and when she took it, he let out a long sigh as he helped her up. At least she was willing to let him touch her.

But her next comment was far from reassuring.

"You should have told me," she said in a strangled voice. "Before we made love, you should have told me what kind of creature you were."

The word creature stung, and he wanted to tell her to take him or leave him. But of course those were words he simply couldn't utter. Instead he tried to make her understand what he was feeling. "I was in love with you," he said in a voice he couldn't quite hold steady, "and I was terrified that you would walk away from me. If you want to call that 'taking the coward's way out,' go ahead."

He saw a raft of expressions chase themselves across her face, and he thought for a moment that she might reach for him. Instead she turned away.

Behind him someone cleared his throat. It was Cole. "Are you all right?"

"Yeah, thanks to you guys." He gestured toward the body on the floor. "It seems Denato wasn't dead. Apparently he and Freemont had plots and counterplots. I guess Denato was going to take the money and disappear. Freemont must have realized he needed a way to find Denato's stash.

"Denato was waiting for Tory to come back and get the loot. He thought she was working with Freemont. Nice guys."

The other werewolf eyed the way Brand and Tory stood stiffly in the confined space.

"We were barricaded in here," Brand clipped out. "There was only one way I could take him down."

Cole knelt beside the body. "He died of a gunshot wound."

"Good," Brand said.

Tory was staring at Cole. She looked from him to Brand and back again. "At the Refuge, I heard an animal growl in back of Freemont. You said it was you."

"Yeah."

"You said you were good at making animal sounds."

"I am."

"Like Brand is?" she clarified.

"Yes."

"You said you were married."

"Yes. Very happily married," he answered, obviously giving her an unspoken message. "For the record, Emma found out about me the way you found out about Brand. And I don't wear a ring because it would mangle my paw."

Brand saw Tory press her hands against her sides and take several deep breaths. Looking at Ben, she asked. "Are you one, too?"

"No. But I touch dead people and get their last memories."

"What?"

"Most Decorah agents have special talents."

Nick cleared his throat. "If I focus my concentration, I can make myself disappear."

Tory nodded slowly, taking in a lot of information at once.

"We should get out of here," Cole said.

"After we get the money," Brand answered. "Denato told us where to find it."

Tory stared at him. "We're going to keep it?"

"Yeah, Decorah can do a lot of good with it. We might as well stuff it in some of those gourmet popcorn boxes."

Brand turned and walked back to the bedroom, thinking he'd wanted to tell Tory about the wolf in private. Instead there had been a whole lot of witnesses to her reaction.

With a grimace, he started banging his heel against the floorboards until he found a hollow place.

"Bring me a knife from the kitchen," he said to Ben.

When the other agent returned to the bedroom, Brand used the knife to pry up a couple of boards. Inside were cardboard boxes filled with bills in large denominations. Brand riffled through one and whistled. "Looks like half a mil in this one. And we don't even need the popcorn boxes."

Each of the agents took two boxes. Tory looked like she didn't want to touch Denato's money, but she agreed to take another box.

There were still boxes under the floor when Brand put the boards back. "Maybe the people who buy the condo will have a nice surprise."

"What about Denato?" Cole asked. "I mean, what are the cops going to think?"

"I put the gun back in his hand," Nick said. "There's gunshot residue on his hand and bullet holes all over the place. As far as anyone can tell, he was in a gun battle."

"As well as a dogfight," Cole added. "The ME should have fun with that."

Brand looked at Tory who had kept on her gloves. His own were gone, but he wiped down any surfaces he might have touched in the bathroom.

"Kept your head down," Brand reminded Tory as they took the elevator to the basement level and returned to the van.

She answered with a small nod.

He wanted to take her aside and have it out with her, but he knew that would have to wait until after they flew back to Beltsville.

In the van, Nick called Frank to report that they were safely out of the condo—and that they were bringing a little present from the Big Apple. He skipped any details that they'd be discussing at Decorah headquarters.

There was a minimum of conversation on the trip back. None of the other guys dared to make any comments about the frozen silence between Brand and Tory.

He kept glancing at her, alternating between wanting to pull her into his arms and wanting to bang his head against the bulkhead. This was his fault. She was right. He should have come clean with her.

When they arrived at Decorah headquarters, Frank came out to meet them. Brand glanced at the other men. "Can you report? Tory and I have to talk."

"Yes," Cole answered.

Brand turned to her. "There are private rooms in the back."

At least she followed him inside to one of the lounges where the staff could relax. He closed the door, thinking about locking it but deciding that was probably going too far at the moment.

"You have something to say?" Tory asked.

"What I'd like to do is take you back to the safe house and fuck your eyeballs out until you acknowledge how good we are together."

"That's a great way to describe making love. Is that how a werewolf cements the relationship between him and his mate?" she shot back.

"In olden times. Now he talks to her, too."

"And what are you offering me, exactly?" she asked.

"A husband who ..."

"Husband," she interrupted. "You said I was your lifemate."

"Yes. But I'm not going to chain you in a cave. We'd be married. Like Cole and Emma," he said. "Or my cousin Ross and his wife, Megan."

"Tell me about Cole and Emma."

"His wife is a Decorah agent. But she's pregnant now and on leave."

He could see Tory digesting this information.

"You could talk to her," he said.

"First I want to talk to you. Everything between us happened so fast. I felt like I was drawn to you in a way I couldn't understand. Is that because you worked some, . ." She stopped and swallowed. "Some werewolf magic on me?"

He clenched and unclenched his hands, ordering himself not to reach for her. Not yet.

"I'll try to explain. When a werewolf gets to be around thirty, the urge to find a mate is very strong. I was fighting it, thinking that I liked my freedom. Then I saw you, and I knew …"

She interrupted him. "So it's hormones or something. You compelled me to want you."

"Or it's like any two people who meet and know they were destined to be together. If you want to call that hormones, you can."

"And just how many of you are there?"

"I don't know. I just know about the Marshall clan. Or maybe we're the only ones. We're descended from a Druid priest who asked the gods for spccial powers. And this is what he got. There aren't many of us because …" It was his turn to stop and swallow. "Because not many of us lived. It's a sex-linked trait, so only male children survived."

She kept her gaze on him. "You're saying that if I got pregnant with a girl, she'd die?"

"Ross's wife, Megan, is a geneticist who has fixed that problem. And the other problem. It used to be that half of us didn't make it through the first time we changed to wolf form. She came up with a drug combination that got her and

Ross's son through the change. You won't have to lose children the way my mom and my aunts did."

"If I stay with you," she said in a flat voice.

The way she said it made him feel like he was standing on the edge of a cliff, with the ground crumbling under his feet. He could tell her he'd only be half alive if she left him. Maybe she didn't care.

She was looking down at her hands.

He held his breath as long seconds passed. Finally she raised her head. A spark of hope kindled inside him when he saw that her expression had softened.

"I guess while I was being mad at you, I forgot that I'd be dead or insane if you hadn't risked your life to get me away from Dr. Son of a Bitch."

He blinked, then forced himself to say, "You don't have to pay me back for anything."

"No. I think you're right. Something happened between us the first time we saw each other—when I saw that wolf standing below my balcony staring at me. I know you told me, but it's just sinking in that the wolf was you. And maybe fate or the ancient gods sent you to me."

When she took a step forward, he did the same. They reached for each other at the same time, and he clasped her to him, so many emotions surging through him. Relief. Joy. And thankfulness.

"Thank God," he whispered, just before his lips came down hard on hers.

He wanted to be gentle with her. He wanted to show her how civilized a werewolf could be. But urgency compelled him to devour her mouth. Still holding her, he backed up, then reached behind him to click the lock on the door.

The sound made her look up. "We're at your office."

"Yeah. But nobody's going to bother us."

"Won't they know?"

"Do you care?"

She considered the question for a split second before clasping her hands around the back of his head and bringing his mouth back to hers.

He reached for the hem of her shirt, sliding his hands inside so that he could run them over the silky skin of her back, then brought them around to pull her bra out of the way and cup her breasts.

She made a sound of approval as he stroked his thumbs across her nipples.

"Brand. Please, I can't wait."

He fumbled for the button at the top of her jeans while she did the same for him. He kicked his pants away and carried her to the sofa where he laid her down and covered her body with his.

She cried out as he came into her, then cried out again as she climaxed. And he was right there with her, plunging off a cliff into free fall. But she was there to catch him in her arms.

They clung together, rocking, kissing, and hugging.

"I'm sorry I didn't tell you," he whispered. "I knew I had to do it."

"I understand why it was so hard." She raised her head to look him in the eye. "Because I know how panicked I'd be if I thought I was going to lose you."

Her confession was like a balm to his soul, and he gathered her close. "Never."

She stayed in his arms for long minutes, then glanced toward the door. "Maybe we should get dressed."

He was pretty sure nobody was going to come knocking, but he got up and pulled his pants on, and she put herself back together, then stood looking at him.

"What?"

"I still don't exactly understand what happened with Freemont and Denato. It was Freemont's men who took me up to the Refuge?"

"Yes. Freemont must have started keeping close tabs on Denato. I think Freemont thought Denato really had been

202

murdered—and this was the ideal time to get information out of you, since you'd be shaken by witnessing the murder of your boyfriend."

She snorted. "I was shaken, but not because he was my boyfriend."

Brand nodded. "When a body didn't turn up, I'm thinking Freemont started thinking Denato had pulled a fast one—and it was even more important to get you to rat him out."

Her gaze turned inward. "That makes some kind of sense. But today we went into Denato's apartment. Why couldn't Freemont do that?"

"We got in because Denato wanted to set a trap for us. Well, for you. Freemont wasn't going to take that kind of chance without good reason. He knew the place would be guarded if Denato was still around. He wanted specific information before he risked anything. I'm also guessing that Denato didn't know Freemont had kidnapped you."

She nodded. "Okay, maybe all of that makes sense."

"If you're a mobster with no moral fiber," Brand answered.

She still looked uncertain. "You said the place was guarded. Why did Denato come in alone?"

"I guess he thought he was only going up against a ditz brain dancer and her friend."

"Yeah."

Brand glanced toward the locked door. "Do you want to stay here and maybe order steak sandwiches? I can ditch the bread. Or I can have steak, and you can order a pizza."

She laughed. "You mean hole up in here until everyone else leaves?"

"If you're still worried about what they might think."

"I am—a little," she admitted as she turned to the mirror and finger combed her hair. "But staying here would make me feel like a coward."

"We both know you're not. Not after the way I've seen you handle yourself."

She reached for his hand. "Okay, we'll go out there—so your friends can stop worrying about us."

"I think they know we've worked things out—either that or killed each other."

She snorted, then raised her chin. "We'll be proud and unapologetic—the way we're going to live the rest of our lives."

Her words and the look on her face warmed him, and he thanked the ancient gods that he had traveled north to find this amazing woman.

THE END

AFTERWORD

Thank you for purchasing HUNTING MOON, I hope you enjoyed reading it as much as I loved writing it.

If you enjoy my books, do me a huge favor. Please go back to www.amazon.com, and leave an honest review. Authors live and die by their reviews. The few extra seconds it takes are really appreciated. Thank you!

DECORAH SECURITY SERIES
(sexy paranormal romantic suspense)
BY REBECCA YORK

#1. ON EDGE (e-book novella and Decorah prequel).

#2. DARK MOON (e-book and trade paperback novel).

#3. CHAINED (e-book novella).

#4. AMBUSHED (e-book short story).

#5. DARK POWERS (e-book and trade paperback novel).

#6. HOT AND DANGEROUS (e-book short story).

#7. AT RISK (e-book and trade paperback novel).

#8. CHRISTMAS CAPTIVE (e-book novella).

#9. DESTINATION WEDDING (e-book novella).

#10. RX MISSING (e-book and trade paperback novel)

#11 HUNTING MOON (e-book and trade paperback novel).

#12 TERROR MANSION (e-book novella).

DECORAH SECURITY COLLECTION (e-book including *Ambushed, Hot and Dangerous, Chained,* and *Dark Powers*).

OFF-WORLD SERIES
(sexy science-fiction romance)
BY REBECCA YORK

#1. HERO'S WELCOME (e-book romance short story).

#2. NIGHTFALL (e-book romance novella).

#3. CONQUEST (e-book romance short story).

#4. ASSIGNMENT DANGER (e-book romance novella).

#5. CHRISTMAS HOME (e-book romance short story).

#6. FIRELIGHT CONFESSION (e-book romance novella).

OFF WORLD COLLECTION (e-book including *Nightfall, Hero's Welcome,* and *Conquest*).

PRAISE FOR REBECCA YORK

Rebecca York delivers page-turning suspense.
—Nora Roberts

Rebecca York never fails to deliver. Her strong characterizations, imaginative plots and sensuous love scenes have made fans of thousands of romance, romantic suspense and thriller readers.
—Chassie West

Rebecca York will thrill you with romance, kill you with danger and chill you with the supernatural.
—Patricia Rosemoor

(Rebecca York) is a real luminary of contemporary series romance
—Michael Dirda, The Washington Post Book World

Rebecca York's writing is fast-paced, suspenseful, and loaded with tension.
—Jayne Ann Krentz

ABOUT REBECCA YORK

A New York Times and USA Today Best-Selling Author, Rebecca York is a 2011 recipient of the Romance Writers of America Centennial Award. Her career has focused on romantic suspense, often with paranormal elements.

Her 16 Berkley books and novellas include her nine-book werewolf "Moon" series. KILLING MOON was a launch book for the Berkley Sensation imprint. She has written for Harlequin, Berkley, Dell, Tor, Carina Press, Silhouette, Kensington, Running Press, Tudor, Pageant Books, and Scholastic.

Her many awards include two Rita finalist books. She has two Career Achievement awards from Romantic Times: for Series Romantic Suspense and for Series Romantic Mystery. And her Peregrine Connection series won a Lifetime Achievement Award for Romantic Suspense Series.

Many of her novels have been nominated for or won RT Reviewers Choice awards. In addition, she has won a Prism Award, several New Jersey Romance Writers Golden Leaf awards and numerous other awards.

Rebecca York loves to hear from readers!

Web site: http://www.rebeccayork.com
Email: rebecca@rebeccayork.com
Twitter: @rebeccayork43
Facebook: http://www.facebook.com/ruthglick
Blog: http://www.rebeccayork.blogspot.com

Sign up for Rebecca York's Newsletter to get all the scoop on Rebecca's
SEXY ROMANTIC SUSPENSE at
http://rebeccayork.com/for-readers/newsletter-sign-up/